Cutthroat Mafia 2

Ghost

**Lock Down Publications and Ca$h
Presents**
Cutthroat Mafia 2
A Novel by *Ghost*

Ghost

Lock Down Publications
P.O. Box 944
Stockbridge, Ga 30281

Visit our website @
www.lockdownpublications.com

Copyright 2020 by Ghost
Cutthroat Mafia 2

First Edition September 2020
Printed in the United States of America

This is a work of fiction. Names, characters, places, and incidents either are products of the author's imagination or are used fictitiously. Any similarity to actual events or locales or persons, living or dead, is entirely coincidental.

Lock Down Publications
Like our page on Facebook: Lock Down Publications @
www.facebook.com/lockdownpublications.ldp
Cover design and layout by: **Dynasty Cover Me**
Book interior design by: **Shawn Walker**
Edited by: **Lashonda Johnson**

Stay Connected with Us!

Text **LOCKDOWN** to 22828 to stay up-to-date with new releases, sneak peaks, contests and more…
Thank you.

Submission Guideline.

Submit the first three chapters of your completed manuscript to ldpsubmissions@gmail.com, subject line: Your book's title. The manuscript must be in a .doc file and sent as an attachment. Document should be in Times New Roman, double spaced and in size 12 font. Also, provide your synopsis and full contact information. If sending multiple submissions, they must each be in a separate email.

Have a story but no way to send it electronically? You can still submit to LDP/Ca$h Presents. Send in the first three chapters, written or typed, of your completed manuscript to:

LDP: Submissions Dept
P.O. Box 944
Stockbridge, Ga 30281

DO NOT send original manuscript. Must be a duplicate.

Provide your synopsis and a cover letter containing your full contact information.

Thanks for considering LDP and Ca$h Presents.

Dedications:

First of all, this book is dedicated to my Baby Girl 3/10, the love of my life and purpose for everything I do. As long as I'm alive, you'll never want nor NEED for anything. We done went from flipping birds to flipping books. The best is yet to come.

To LDP'S CEO- Ca$h & COO- Shawn:

I would like to thank y'all for this opportunity. The wisdom, motivation, and encouragement that I've received from you two is greatly appreciated.

The grind is real. The loyalty in this family is real. I'm riding with LDP 'til the wheels fall off.

THE GAME IS OURS !

Ghost

Chapter 1

Kayley laid on her back with her eyes closed and tried to drift off to sleep for the third time, but no matter how hard she tried, she couldn't escape to the dream world that she knew she so desperately needed to be in. Her mind was restless. Her every thought was of Preston. She worried about the kind of trouble Macho was about to lead him into. No matter how much Preston wanted to do the right thing, or how much she fought to pull Preston out of the game she knew that as long as he was attached to Macho that the task would be nearly impossible. This fact drove her absolutely crazy. She pulled the silky sheets over her head and tried once again to drift off. She thought about Marco, and how he'd looked laid out on the floor after she'd lost her cool and ended his life after he'd forced himself on her. Images of his pain-stricken face and the guttural noises that he made when the knife slammed into his heart plagued her conscience. She shook her head and threw the covers off her body, before sitting up and planting her back against the headboard.

"Damn, when does this remorseful shit end? I'm tired of seeing him in my dreams. He brought his own death on himself, Lord. He got what he deserved. You know it, and so do I. Please help me to forget about him. I'm tired of having the nightmares, and the sick feeling that resonates deep within my gut. I just wanna be free. Please release me from the bondage of his murder. Please," Kayley prayed with her eyes wide open.

She sat there for a moment, then slid back down into the bed, pulling the sheets back over her body, and then her head. She closed her eyes and swallowed the lump inside her throat. She remained that way for five full minutes. Her mind began to wander aimlessly. Slowly she started to drift off, a slight smoke crossed her faces before a sudden noise caused her to kick her legs violently. She sat up holding her breath.

"Hello?" Her eyebrows furrowed.

She slid her right hand under the pillow that Preston laid his head on. She wrapped her hand around the handle of a .45 automatic with a tactical silencer on the end of it. It was already cocked, locked, and loaded. Her left hand rested on her baby bump. She listened more intently.

Amir's two trained killers slowly stepped into the hotel's bedroom standing beside one another with black ski masks over their faces and dressed in all black from head to toe. They held deer hunting knives in their hands, and one of them a roll of silver duct tape. He stepped forward to the foot of Kayley's bed.

He pulled a strip of tape from the roll. "Say, baby, we don't want to hurt you. But we don't have any problem doing it if you don't play ball. Now we have our orders and they are for you to come with us, right now," he hissed, placing the knife back into the sheath that was inside of his jacket. He took a hold of the sheet and slowly began to pull it off, Kayley.

Kayley tightened her hand around the barrel of Preston's gun. "P-p-please get out of here. I don't want any trouble. How did you get in here?"

The killer that stood closest to the foot of the bed stuck out his tongue and licked the length of the long-serrated blade of the knife. "Listen to me, baby girl. We can do this two ways. The first way is, you can come with us peacefully, and soundly. Or I can personally slit your throat and throw you over my shoulder with blood gushing out of you like a geyser. Either way, the end result will be the same you will submit to your destiny." He dared to place a knee on the bed causing the springs to squeak.

"We gotta hurry up and get this bitch," the other killer said, frowning under his mask.

The first killer reached to grab a hold of Kayley's ankle. She screamed and kicked at him. He raised his knife with the intention of stabbing her in the thigh to show her that he meant business. Kayley saw the blade raise and for her, it was like everything began to move in slow motion. The blade came down and sunk into her right thigh, the killer pulled it out and was about to come down with it again. Kayley screamed for a second time. She came from under the pillow with the silenced .45. She aimed and fired three shots back to back to back.

The first bullet zipped from the barrel of the gun and burned a hole directly in the center of the stabbing killer's forehead, thick chunks of his brain flew out the back of his head and wound up on the carpet behind him. He blinked twice before his eyes crossed. He wound up on the carpet with his eyelids wide open. Kayley hopped up with the barrel of the gun smoking. She shook from the sheer shock of what had transpired before her.

The second killer tackled her into the headboard and caused her to holler out in pain. Air from her lungs came out of her in a loud whoosh. She felt immediate pain in her stomach. The killer punched her twice in the face and flung her to the ground. He raised his black boot and stomped her as hard as he could in the stomach, then fell on top of her raining down blow after blow.

"You silly bitch! That was my brother! You killed my fuckin' brother!" he hollered punching her over and over.

Kayley passed out for a second and woke up with his fists raining down on her. She took the gun and began to pull the trigger over and over. The first bullet missed. The second one whizzed past the killer's head. The third one lodged into his chin. He hollered out in serious pain. The fourth, fifth, and sixth bullets found a home in his chest. The seventh burrowed into his left eye. He flew backward shaking. Kayley jumped up with blood leaking from between her thighs. She stood over him, and dumped him down three more times, before she staggered backward, dizzy, and disoriented. She collapsed on the carpet with the river of both killer's blood forming a puddle around her body.

***

Macho was halfway out of the parking lot, after gunning down Pooh when something told him to look into his rearview mirror. Upon doing so, he saw Lashonda fall out of the back window fully engulfed in flames. She had her arms in the air with the intense fire cooking her to death. She screamed and patted the flames. She turned around in a half-circle before she fell to her knees face first and shook until her life left her body. Macho's eyes grew as big as saucers. He started to panic.

He threw his whip in reverse and sped backward until he slammed on the brakes right in front of a deceased, Lashonda. He jumped out of his vehicle and rushed to her side. The scent of burnt skin and flesh resonated prominently in the atmosphere. He kneeled and took two full minutes to pat out her flames while the G Wagon's fire grew higher and higher. He grabbed Lashonda to him, tears fell from his eyes. She was so hot that she burned him.

He dropped her. "Aw shit, Shorty. Aw shit, I didn't know you were with him. I swear to God I didn't know." He tried to pick her up again.

Her face was wrinkled and a bloody pink. She was no longer, common sense told him this. He dropped her back to the ground and thought about Lashawn while scanning the parking lot of the apartment complex to see if he could locate any witnesses. When none were visible, he stood up and left Lashonda on the ground lifeless.

"I fucked up. Damn, I fucked up." The heat of the burning Wagon caused his ski mask to itch horribly. He ignored it, and jogged back to his whip, storming out of the parking lot with tears running down his face and along his neck.

***

Preston cruised scanning the dark Baltimore streets. He hit Macho's phone for the thirtieth time and grew irritated. He didn't like to feel ignored. He'd been driving around looking for his right-hand man for over two hours and had come up with nothing. He was frustrated and feeling defeated. He waited for the phone to go to voicemail before he set it back in his lap and continued to cruise. His eyelids were getting heavy. He sat up straight and kept driving.

"Yo, I'm getting sleepy. I gotta turn in before I fuck around and slam into somethin'." He jumped on the highway and headed back toward the hotel doing seventy-five miles an hour with the window down so that the air could help him to stay awake. He prayed that Kayley was asleep. He didn't feel like arguing with her about him having to leave and go find Macho. He understood her stance, but he just didn't want to hear it. "I'm on my way back, Goddess. Please be sleep."

***

Lashawn drove into the parking lot wildly and slammed on the brakes of her Chevy Corsica. She jumped out of it and ran toward the yellow tape. Policemen were all over the parking lot along with two fire trucks, and two ambulances. She looked across the tape and saw Pooh and Lashonda's bodies covered with white sheets. There were evidence markers everywhere. She looked to her right and saw Pooh's G Wagon on its side and burned black. Now she was really nervous.

She lifted the tape and ran toward the bodies. Her friend Lisa had hit her up on Facebook saying that Pooh had been gunned down and sat on fire and that she was sure Lashonda was with him. After Lashawn called and confirmed that her daughter was no longer with Pooh's mother and that Pooh had picked her up, she feared the worst. Before she could make it all the way to the bodies, she was accosted by three police officers. They tackled her to the ground.

"Let me go! Please! I need to know if that is my daughter under that sheet. She was with him!" she screamed.

"Ma'am, you can't trample the scene. This is a murder investigation and every tad bit of evidence is crucial," he told her flexing his muscles to keep her pinned.

Lashawn struggled against him. "Please, just lift the sheet. That's all I want you to do. Just lift the smaller one," she cried.

"Can you promise me that you won't trample the crime scene?" He continued to hold her firmly.

She nodded. "Yes, I promise. Please."

Three minutes later she stood a safe distance behind the yellow tape. When the lead detective of the investigation pulled back the sheet and revealed that it was in fact, Lashonda, Lashawn fell to her knees in disbelief. She couldn't scream. All she could do was shake her head over and over with tears running.

"Why would this happen to my baby, Lord? How could this happen? She is just a child." She covered her face with her hands and broke down like never before. Her friend Lisa came to console her, but it was of no use. Lashawn was lost, shattered, and emotionally dismantled.

14

***

Preston stepped into his hotel room and was about to avoid turning on the lights when he stepped on the carpet that was drenched in blood. He raised his Jordan and looked down at the white sole that was now covered in blood.

"What the fuck?" He flipped on the lights, and his heart sank when he caught sight of the two slain killers.

They looked as if they'd been executed by terrorists. His eyes scanned the room. When they landed on Kayley, he saw the blood between her thighs and cursed under his breath.

"Fuck, baby girl!" He rushed to her and picked her up. She was knocked out cold from the brutal beating by the second killer, and the unfortunate blood lost. He tapped her face. "Baby, baby, wake up. Wake up, bae." Kayley was unmoving.

Preston felt his heart skip a beat. He carried her to the bed and got on the phone. He needed the room cleaned, the killers disposed of, and he needed to get Kayley to a hospital at once before he could put the pieces of the puzzle together that would tell him who had attacked them. His mind was racing so fast that he became dizzy. His clean up man picked up the phone, and their business to get things in order commenced.

Ghost

Chapter 2

It was a dark and gloomy Thursday evening when Lashawn laid her six-year-old daughter Lashonda to rest. She stood over the open grave as the Reverend lowered Lashonda's casket into the ground. LaShawn's mascara trailed down her cheeks like streaks of mud. Her nose hurt because she was all sniffled out. She growled one last time and released the final bit of excruciating, psychological pain into the atmosphere that had kept her bound and grief-stricken over the past ten days consecutively.

Macho held the umbrella over her head and allowed the rain to pelt down onto it. He slipped his right arm around her waist and rested his cheek against hers. "Baby, are you okay?"

Lightning flashed across the expanse of the sky, then ten seconds later there was a loud rumbling from up above before Lashawn had a chance to respond. Macho swallowed again. He felt sick to his stomach and had yet to find the space to admit his transgressions that had caused the death of Lashonda. The guilt was killing him.

Lashawn turned around to face him. "They don't give a fuck about us, Macho. It's going on two weeks, and they still ain't found out who did this shit to my child. I swear to God it ain't right. I need some answers. This shit is tearing me apart."

Lightning flashed once again, the audio of the rainfall attacking the graveyard was boisterous, followed by the roar from the sky. Macho rubbed the side of LaShawn's face and avoided her eyes. "I got every killa on the payroll looking for these clowns. The recovery fee is a million dollars, that's money that I ain't even got yet, but I'ma get it. Baby, I promise you as soon as they find whoever did this I'ma cut their head off and bring it to you in a Ziploc bag."

Lashawn shook her head. "No, you not. When you find whoever took my daughter away from me, you're going to bring me to them, and you're going to let me enjoy the satisfaction of taking them off this earth. I wanna make their mother feel how I'm feeling right now because it ain't fair. Who would do such a thing to a beautiful little girl? She was just a child. I should've never let her go with Pooh. It wasn't even his week to have her, I made an exception, and it cost me my daughter's life." She broke down and fell to her knees. Mud gushed into her black stockings.

Macho fell on his knees beside her. He placed his arm around her shoulder. "I'm sorry, baby. I'm so so sorry. I don't know exactly what you're feeling right now but you need to know that seeing you hurt is killing me. You are my everything. I can't cope knowing that you are in this unmistakable pain."

Lashawn turned her head and cried hard into his chest. "I just wanna wake up and find out that this is a terrible nightmare. I can't live without my baby. I hate Pooh so much. I swear to God I do."

Macho rubbed her back and tilted his head toward the sky. The rain fell into his face and rolled down his neck. He lowered his head and held Lashawn as close to himself as he could. "Baby, let's get out of here. I wanna get you home so I can cater to you a lil' bit. I wanna give you a bath, and oil you down. Then I'ma lay you in bed and hold you. You can tell me anything that's on your heart and I'ma listen for as long as you need me to. I love you, Lashawn. I'ma hold you down, that's my word." He slowly helped her onto her feet.

At this time the rain was coming down so hard that their visibility was minimal. Lashawn took one last look into Lashonda's grave before she leaned into Macho and allowed him to lead her to the parking lot, and to his Benz truck. He helped her climb into the passenger's seat and closed the door behind her. Macho got in and fixed her seat belt across her chest. Lashawn was stuck, everything still felt so surreal.

Macho sat there for a moment with the windshield wipers on high. They swished from side to side. His stomach was in knots. He wanted so desperately to tell Lashawn what had taken place between him and Pooh, but how could he? How could he explain that he was responsible for her daughter burning to death? How could he tell her that he was the killer in question? What would a confession from him look like? How would things be directly afterward?

He didn't know. He couldn't imagine it and because he couldn't he decided against the moment to admit anything. Instead, he pulled out of the graveyard, and away from Lashawn's source of pain. He couldn't help eyeing her from the side of his face. He knew it would be impossible for him to keep the truth from her forever. Sooner or later he would have to face her with the truth. It was just in him to do so.

***

Preston scooted to the edge of the couch and picked up Kayley's brown teddy bear. He held it in his big hands looking it over. It was seven o'clock at night and storming terribly outside of their apartment. He shook his head and took a deep breath. He looked over at Kayley as she poured herself another round of Hennessey. She was already a bit tipsy.

"Yo, I hope you know that you can't drown your troubles away with all that drinking. Sooner or later we are going to have to face this reality."

Kayley downed half the glass and ran her fingers through her thick, curly hair. She looked across the table at him and downed the rest of it before slamming the glass on the table.

"Okay, Preston, you wanna do this? Let's do it. What do you want me to say?" Her right eye was still slightly blackened. When she spoke, her jaw felt vulnerable from her attack.

"First thing you gotta know is that I ain't the enemy. I'm ya man, and I'm standing behind you one hunnit percent. Ain't no reason for us to be beefing with one another, especially when right now we are all that we have."

Kayley smacked her lips. "Boy, please. You don't think I've been seeing the way you've been looking at me ever since we found out I lost our baby, huh, Preston? You don't think that I can tell that your love toward me is different? Your touch, your embraces, your speech, all of it is different!" She grabbed the bottle of Hennessey and filled her glass.

Preston came over and sat beside her. "Yo, hand to God, you're bugging. You making it seem like I think it's your fault that you were attacked. I ain't that stupid, Kayley. If there is a reason that it feels like I am acting differently it's because I feel guilty, baby. I know damn well that whoever did this shit to us was trying to clap at me, and this is how they came. They killed my niece and my child."

"Our child, Preston. It ain't just about you, it's about us. They fucked us both over." She downed the entire glass and slammed it on the table. "And you wanna know what makes it so bad?"

Preston grabbed the bottle and twisted the cap back on it. "What's that, shorty?"

"I really wanted this baby. You are the first man that I looked forward to having a baby with. Now I feel like I've lost that special opportunity. I feel so broken." She scooted back on the couch and tossed her head back.

"Yo, you talking like we ain't still together or somethin'. They might've taken our child for the moment, but we are still here and we ain't gon' let nobody break us." He felt himself getting vexed.

"It's too late. From the moment the doctor told me that I was no longer with child, my soul has felt empty. I can't think straight. I don't know where to begin. On top of that, those two dudes that I killed are plaguing me with remorseful dreams. I'm scared to sleep because their souls are haunting me." She closed her eyes.

That was a real thing. Every killa knew that your first couple murders were always the ones that seemed to do the most psychological damage. Whenever you slept the victims showed up, begging, pleading, and asking you why you killed them? Oftentimes, they caused you to become paralyzed while you slept. The old heads called it a witch riding your back, or the spirits that hadn't crossed over quite yet seeking their last feasible revenge against you.

Preston wrapped her in his arms and kissed her forehead. "That's gon' pass, baby. I have been through that stage and I promise you it passes. When it does, you'll feel a million times better, and hopefully, we'll be able to move on with our lives. We can't allow for this moment to break us."

"I wish I was as strong as you, but you have no idea how it felt to feel that child nourishing itself from my body. I felt complete. I felt needed and special. I mean I know that you and I are going to always be together but it's common sense to know that we are going to go through our ups and downs and that there will be times when we hate each other, and the love will be questionable on both ends. With my child, it doesn't matter what I go through with it, my baby will always love me, against all odds. I'm hurting right now, and the only thing that's healing me is Mrs. Hennessey. Now give me the damn bottle."

Preston held it out of her reach. "N'all, shorty. The doctor said you need to take it easy. You can't drown your cares away in a bottle. You gotta be careful."

"Yo' fuck off. Give me that bottle, kid before you get me turnt." She sat up and reached for it.

Preston stood with it in his hands. "You had enough. I'm cutting yo' ass off. Chill with the buzz you got and get ya mind right. I don't like this side of you. You are stronger than this."

"Stronger than this?" She glared at him and bounced to her feet. "Preston, if you don't stop playing wit' me I'ma show you why they say that everything is bigger in Texas, because I'ma out these size sevens up yo' ass and they gon' magically expand. Now, give me the fuckin' bottle! I ain't playin' wit' yo' ass."

Preston twisted the top off the bottle and turned it upside down spilling the contents on the floor. He mugged her while he did this. The liquor popped off the floor and all over the bottom of the couch until he was done pouring. When he finished, he tried to hand her the bottle. "Huh."

Kayley smacked it out of his hand. It landed against the wall and broke into pieces. She stormed into his face. "Preston, I swear to God, sometimes you make me wanna get all up in yo' ass. You lucky I love you, but I swear, I can't look at you, right now. Why don't you go and take a drive? Go find out who did this to our child. I don't wanna see you no more tonight." She mugged him for a few seconds, then bumped him and headed out of the room slamming the bedroom door behind her.

As soon as she left Preston, flopped onto the couch shaking his head. "This girl gon' drive me crazy. Yo', Jehovah please give me the strength, man, word up."

***

Macho leaned back his seat as the new Roddy Rich LP crooned out of his speakers. He puffed on a big blunt and had a bottle of Lean between his thighs. He was already high off Codeine and Robitussin. He'd just popped two Percocets and headed for the third. He was itching, and fiending to escape his internal pains. He inhaled four more puffs and passed his blunt to Preston.

Preston was dozing off against the window of Macho's Benz truck. He was lit off Lean and pink Mollies. He took the blunt and puffed it five times, then handed it back to Macho. He sipped from his dirty Sprite that consisted of three Percocet Sixties, a pink tablet of Mollie, and Lean. His throat was scratchy, and his eyelids felt like they were being pulled down by a bodybuilder on steroids.

"Yo', my bitch driving me crazy, Kid. I know she is hurting, and all of that shit, but the God ain't the enemy." Preston nodded out for a second and slowly came back to his senses keeping his eyes closed.

Macho woke up from his own slumber and wiped his face with his hands. "I understand where you're coming from, Slime. Yo, Lashawn been wilding out for obvious reasons. I mean, I get what a loss like that could do for any mother so I ain't tripping. I just don't know what to do."

Preston had a heavy heart for his niece and sister. "I ain't been able to touch bases wit' her, son. I know she fucked up. That was her baby, nah mean? That nigga Pooh had so many enemies that I don't even know where to begin. It ain't like I can go and hit up none of his Payroll homies for no help. According to the streets, they thought that our Cutthroat Mafia had something to do with Pooh's death. And after briefing the entire crew on my end, that doesn't seem to be the case. What about on your side?" Preston got comfortable on the couch and closed his eyes.

Macho felt weighed down with grief. He dropped his head into his lap and shook it from right to left. "Nah,' kid, ain't none of the homies take credit for slumping that fool yet. Besides, any hits from the crew have to come across my desk first. Pooh ain't got an on-sight order on his life before he got killed. I felt like placing one on it, but I didn't."

"Well, that puts us back to square one, kid. Fuck we gon' do?" Preston rubbed his nose and started to scratch his arm. The Percocets were starting to bother him something fierce.

Macho shrugged his shoulders as the image of Lashonda running out of the G Wagon on fire played before his mind's eye. He hurriedly shook the image from his head. "Yo', we gotta keep combing the slums. Ain't shit else we can do. We gotta tear this bitch up if that's what it calls for." He threw his head back.

A tear threatened to seep from his closed lids. He thought about hugging Lashonda again. He imagined the pain that Lashawn was going through as a mother. His heart felt as heavy as an anvil. He needed to change the subject. "Yo', what's good wit, Kayley? Shorty a'ight?"

"N'all, Blood, she's losing it. She said she really wanted that baby that she lost. Every minute of the day she is drinking and shit. I can only imagine trying to wash away the pain. It's bananas, I try and console her but she ain't fuckin' wit' me. I'm more lost than a kid's mitten at recess, word up."

"Preaching to the choir, son, straight the fuck up. I think the only thing we can do is get back to the money and keep our revenge at the forefront of our brains. The Rebirth been taking off like a forest fire. We dumping three kilos a day, and the more the young hittas in the crew crush the other dope boys the more clientele we get from all over the city and surrounding cities. Yo', we dumped two of the bricks to more than thirty hypes that took the drive from Philly and D.C. I'm thinking about opening up shop on some serious shit up in both cities, what you think?"

Preston stood up. "I think it sounds good. Yo', the God gotta hit the bricks. I ain't trying to inflame Kayley even more than I already have. Blood, keep ya head up and stay woke. Got plenty of snakes out here lurking."

Macho slid his hand under the couch and came up with a Mach-90 with a hundred round clip. "Dats why I keep a bad bitch wit' me, nah mean?" He lowered his eyes. "I'ma have a car follow you. Until we find out who's attacking the mob we on high alert. The threat assessment is at red. Hold ya head kid, love."

"Suwoo," Preston called and left out into the night feeling lazy and slow.

Ghost

Chapter 3

It took a full month after all the tragedies before Macho had their operations back up and running at full speed. He opened trap houses all up and down Colgate Avenue and Willow Spring Road that boxed in St. Helena Park where most of the addicts of Dundalk flooded. Whenever out of town addicts came to the city the first area they located was St. Helena Park. Because the area was known for its narcotics, Macho made sure he had troops in place all around to protect his dope boys and his traps. All up and down the strips young, cold-hearted savages from the Cutthroat Mafia strolled along the expanse of the neighborhood with bloody rags hanging out of their right pockets.

The females made sure their hairstyles included a red bandana, and that they also found a way to represent the clique. Macho stood at the top of the throne, and the young savages both male and female honored him as if he was their king. They pledged their loyalties to him and were ready to die for him. In exchange for their loyalties, Macho made sure that their entire households ate good. He paid their bills and kept money in their pockets, and designer clothes draped across their backs.

He kept them armed with top-notch weapons and insured a deadly family value within. At the same time, he made them prejudiced against other crews. He instilled a strong hatred within them for anybody that was getting money in the city outside of the Cutthroat Mafia. Because of this nearly, all the members of his crew took upon a lunatic's mentality. They had a habit of rolling up on their oppositions, hopping out, and stripping them bare, before they riddled them with slugs in a relentless fashion. They slayed with no mercy and no regard, and Macho condoned their actions because the more rivals his crew got out of the way, the faster Macho was able to make up ground and put trap houses in place.

The money began to come so fast that by the third month after Lashonda's death, Macho had over twenty trap houses spread throughout Baltimore, and Dundalk. Preston had fifteen, and they were picking up new areas every day. Macho's safe house became so cluttered with digital safes that he became nervous. He had five million dollars in cash and didn't know the first thing to do with it. He had so many people to feed, palms to grease, and it was imperative that he kept on sending money back to Montana and Makaroni so that they kept the Rebirth coming his way.

Having so many obligations, and so many things going on around him, he felt like his head was spinning. He fell back on the couch inside the room where two safes were opened, each was stuffed with five hundred thousand dollars. There was another six hundred thousand spread across the table in front of him that needed to be counted, and he'd just plugged in his money machine.

Lashawn came into the room, tired of waiting in the car. When she saw all the money her eyes got bucked. She looked around and then over to Macho.

She dropped her Fendi bag on the floor. "Baby, what the hell is all of this?"

Macho ran his hand over his face. "Our future as soon as I can put all of this shit into perspective." He blew air out of his jaws. "I didn't know that this shit was going to be as brain wrenching as it is. After being in the game for a short minute it's safe to say that making the money is the easiest part."

Lashonda picked up twenty-thousand-dollars and thumbed through it. "Yo', dis looks like every bit of a million dollars. I ain't never seen this much money in my entire life."

Macho smiled. "That's because you ain't never fucked with a boss ass nigga before. Yo', I told you that I had you." He got up and wrapped his arms around her waist. "What do you say? You think you ready to get back on that horse yet?" He rubbed her ass and cuffed it.

Lashawn tensed up when she mentally processed what he was getting at. She came out of his embrace rubbing the backs of her arms, turning her back to him. "N'all, Macho, damn. Are we going to have this same conversation every single day?"

Macho frowned. "Hell, yeah, we are. Damn, I mean when I'ma get some of my lady? I been real patient, Lashawn. I understand you're going through a lot psychologically, that's why I ain't been trying to rush you. But baby, I'm fienin'. I need some pussy." He walked up on her with a smile on his face.

Lashawn once again wiggled out of his arms. "That's the last thing on my mind, Macho. I mean I'm thankful that our test results came back negative an everything like that, but the act of sex is the furthest thing from my brain, right now. I think I'ma be screwed up until they find the person that did this to my child. I know you hate to hear this, but it's the honest to God truth. I get that you're a man, so if you feel like you need to go out and do what you do, then go ahead. That's your right."

"Yo', you my woman. I ain't tryna go out there fuckin' wit no other bitch." He pulled her to him. He brushed her hair out of her beautiful face. "Yo', what you want me to do? You want me to go door to door whacking mafuckas until we come up wit' the nigga that did this shit, huh? You want me to track down every enemy Pooh ever had and clap they ass on the strength? Tell me, boo. What can I do for my lady?"

Lashawn looked up to him with a solemn expression across her face. "I don't know. I guess I just need a little space for a while. Not the kind of space that says that we are apart, but the kind that allows me to find my worth in life once again. I have lost me, and before I can feel sexy enough to lay down with you in my strongest sense of womanhood. I need to get right up here." She tapped on her temple. "Can you respect that?"

Macho eased away from her and sat on the couch. He grabbed the bottle of 1942 and turned it up. He wiped his mouth, and took another swallow, before setting the bottle back down. He grabbed twenty thousand dollars in cash and balled it into a knot. "Yo', I don't know what kind of space you looking for, but here go some cheese to help you figure it out. It ain't much, but you still finna take it. So, bring yo' ass over here and get it."

Lashawn slowly came and stood in front of him. She had no intention of turning down the money. She'd already started buying up property in Dundalk unbeknownst to anybody else, and she wanted to continue to do so. She wanted a future where she didn't have to be dependent. She wanted to feel a sense of accomplishment within her own right, and the loss of Lashonda only ignited this passion even more inside of her. She took the money and stuffed it into the purse she'd picked back up off the floor.

"Thank you, baby. I'm sorry, but you need to know that I am really trying. I'll be back soon. I don't know if I'll be the same Lashawn that you remember but you best believe I am going to try the best. I just need some me time, that's all."

Macho nodded and remembered that the way she was feeling was caused by his carelessness. He sunk his shoulders and drank from his bottle again. "Yo', just let the God know when you want me again until then I'm releasing you, effective immediately." He stood up.

Lashawn wasn't feeling the last part of his statement. She placed her hand on her hip and mugged him. "Excuse you? What do you mean that you're releasing me?"

Macho ran his tongue up and down a blunt of Kush before sparking it. "I gotta let you spread ya wings. I can't keep sitting around and waiting for you to look at me with love and affection again. I gotta get back to the slums in a major way. I love you, but I can't allow this thing you're going through to knock me off of my pivot. When you're ready to come back I'll be ready, until then I'm finna do me." He opened the door to the room and held it open for her. "Come on, let's get up out of here."

Lashawn acted like she was about to walk into the hallway and stopped in front of his face. You talking all this shit about loving me, nigga you don't give a fuck about me, or us, because if you did you wouldn't be hollering this what *I'm going through shit.* It would be what *we* are going through as a team. I lost my fuckin' daughter, Macho. My six-year-old, precious little girl and they haven't found the killer yet. I need closure, and I need some peace within my life. If all you can think about is sex, then yeah, it says a lot about you and how you truly feel for me. Since that's the case, and we're saying what we really see in each other, then let me do this then." She turned back around and grabbed an additional twenty thousand dollars. She rolled it into a knot and stuffed it into her purse along with the other twenty. She looked into his eyes. "Now I'm ready to go." She walked past him, bumping him slightly.

Macho stood with a smile on his face. There was no doubt about it. He loved Lashawn. She had all the makings of a wife to him. She was strong, assertive, beautiful, and as jazzy as he could handle her. He knew that he owed her way more than what the money could ever produce, and he felt that until he was able to bless her with another child that he would never be able to look her in the eyes. That was the worst feeling of all for him. He needed to get back to the money, and he needed to find a bunch of bad bitchez that would help him take his mind off the guilt he felt toward Lashawn, the drugs were only numbing the pain momentarily. Yeah, it was time to get back to the old cold-hearted, savage that was Macho.

Chapter 4

Preston looked over at Kayley as she sat in the passenger's seat of his new black-on-black Hellcat with her hair blowing in the wind. She had a Tech-9 on her lap, and her hand around the handle as if she was looking to cause some serious trouble at any moment.

He squeezed her thigh and stroked her cheek. "You been quiet for a minute, baby, what's good?"

Kayley shook her head. "Oh, nothing. I was just sitting here lost in thought for a second. I think I miss my mother. I wanna take a trip out to Houston real soon to see good ol' Miss Jackie." She smiled. "The whole zoom thing ain't working no more." She adjusted the Tech-9 and nodded her head. "Yeah, that's what I wanna do."

"I support that. Whenever you wanna roll out you already know the kid rolling wit' you. I gotta make sure my baby girl is taken care of at all times. So, I'm wit' you baby." He rubbed her thick thigh and went back to scanning the deadly streets of Baltimore.

It was hot and humid out and because of the Coronavirus pandemic nearly everybody he saw had doctor's masks over their faces, or masks that they'd created themselves. It made it very hard for him to be able to pick apart his enemies from average everyday people, but he was hyper-vigilant.

"I appreciate that baby. I need to work out a couple of last-minute details with my mother and as soon as I get them underway, we'll be hitting the road. Are you sure you wanna go down there, though? Texas has the worst cases of the virus, right now. Aren't you worried about contracting the disease?"

"Yo', if it happens it happens. No matter what, I'ma be beside my jewel if it does. I gotta protect my rib. If you going down there, then so am I. Word up." He leaned over and kissed her cheek.

Kayley couldn't help but stare at him. "Baby, I swear to God I love you more and more every single day. You make me so happy even though we are going through some rough things, right now. I wish I would've never lost your baby. We deserve it so much—" She was quiet for a second. She lowered her head and sighed in emotional pain.

"What I tell you about that, Kayley, huh? Didn't I tell you that it wasn't your fault? And that you need to quit blaming yourself for the fact that two fuck niggaz jumped on you, beat you up, and forced you to lose our kid. At least you bammed they bitch ass. Hand to God the prettiest sight outside of you that I ever saw was of those pussy niggaz with their brains all over the room. Yo', I got a killa for a jewel, and I love that shit. But quit feeling sorry for yourself. Jehovah knows what's good with us. When the time is right, he's gon' let me splash your mountains again and our baby gon' be good this time. Have faith beloved. That's all I ask."

Kayley nodded her head. "It's definitely easier said than done. But by God's will, I will get there." She looked out her window and mugged a group of dope boys that all had a bunch of blue bandanas around their necks.

Preston smiled. "What's good, Goddess? Why you mugging them niggaz?"

Kayley cocked the Tech. "I've been feeling really hateful lately. Didn't you say that since the crew has been eliminating all opps, we been making money hand over fist?"

"Fa show."

Kayley looked back over her shoulder. "Yo', fuck it, spin the block. Let me fan these niggaz down. I mean, why not?"

Preston frowned at her and sat up in his soft leather seat. "You fa real?" He checked his rearview and saw the dope boys running up to multiple cars serving them with crack cocaine. This irritated him.

Kayley rolled her window all the way down. "Yeah, spin the block and watch me drop a few of those punks. I feel like I gotta get this shit out of my system." She took off her seat belt.

"Awright bet, fuck it." Preston spun three blocks and wound up pulling up to the corner where the eight hustlers were standing in front of their trap house nodding their head to music blaring out of a Cadillac Escalade that was parked in front of their bando. "How you wanna do this shit?"

Kayley pulled the red Gucci bandanna up over her nose and lowered her eyes. "Slide along the curb and I'ma drop as many of them as I can. Besides, who knows, they coulda been the ones who sent those dudes to get at us while we were in the hotel a few months back. Let's get 'em."

Preston grabbed a Tech from under his seat and cocked it. He rolled down his window and made a right turn on to their block with the sun beaming. He cruised until he was three houses from their trap.

He situated himself up just a bit and pulled in front of their place. "Get at they asses, Shorty."

Kayley was already out of the window with her Tech. "Suwoo! Cutthroat fuck niggaz!"

Boom! Boom! Boom! Boom!

Preston sat on the edge of his window sill leaning across the top of the car firing back to back. "Cutthroat niggaz!"

The dope boys were taken by surprise. Three were dropped right away. Bullets entered into their chests and smoke emitted from the holes. Two tried to run into the trap house, Kayley wet up their backs with so many holes that it looked like they'd been hit with buck shots. They fell and slid down the steps, and both Preston and Kayley kept bussing.

One disappeared on the side of the house and got away with two shots to his arm. Another two made a run for the fence as they jumped into the air the bullets knocked massive chunks out of their flesh. They wound up against the gate bleeding profusely. Kayley scanned the spot and eased back into her seat satisfied. Since somebody had taken her child away from her all she thought about on a daily basis was bloodshed and revenge. The sight of another's blood gave her momentary satisfaction.

Preston slid back into the driver's seat. "Damn, one of those bitch ass niggaz got away. Fuck!" He threw the car in drive and stormed away from the curb with his chest heaving up and down.

He made a hard right, stepped on the gas, and slammed on the brakes when he got to the alley and saw the one dope boy that had gotten away from the murder scene. He backed up just a bit and turned into the alley flying down it all full speed. When the dope boy saw them coming, he cursed out loud and took off running. Preston sped behind him kicking up rocks and dirty litter that was all over the alley. The car closed in and caught the back of the hustler's shoe. He fell to the pavement and the Hellcat rolled over him as if he were nothing more than a speed bump. Preston slammed on the brakes and looked into his rearview mirror. He saw the hustler fighting to get to his feet. His blue bandanna had fallen from around his neck.

Kayley opened her door and took off running down the alley. She chased the limping dope boy until he got to a fence. She stopped and sprayed him down.

Boom! Boom! Boom! Boom!

The bullets ate up his back one after the other. He slid down the gate with plasma leaking out of him. Kayley pressed the barrel to his forehead. "Mafuckas wanna take my baby away from me, a'ight then, I'm finna make every opps mother feel what I feel!"

Boom! Boom! Boom! His face splattered all over her bandanna.

Preston ran up. "Come on shorty, that fuck nigga dead. Mission accomplished."

Kayley jogged over to him. "N'all, Slime, mission just beginning. Come on."

***

Angela Simms opened the door to her Penthouse suite dressed in a red satin, see-through negligée with the matching robe, she smiled when Macho walked through the doors with a bottle of Ace of Spades in his hand. He reeked of marijuana, and his eyes were glossy from the Mollie and Percocets.

She closed the door behind, took a hold of his hand, and led him to the couch. "Have a seat, baby."

Macho yanked his hand away from her. "Bitch what I tell you about all of that emotion shit? Yo', whenever we touch bases it's strictly bidness. Get it." He slumped on the couch and sat back.

Angela smacked her lips. "Boy, don't ruin my afternoon." She rolled her eyes. "I got something for you." She retrieved a small briefcase from the side of the bed and brought it to Macho. "This is a gift from one of the powers from above. He says that he likes what you're doing so far and that his eyes are on you. This is just a small bonus and a token of his admiration."

Macho took the briefcase and popped it open to reveal a hundred thousand dollars in cash. He picked up a stack of the money and smiled. "What's the strings attached to this shit? Ain't shit free, I already know that."

"Yeah, well in this case it is. You are doing your thing, Macho. You're conquering one slum after the next. You're feeding over a hundred workers and their families. You're greasing palms, and all of your success is taking place so swiftly because you are allowing me to guide you. It takes a lot for a man to set his pride aside so that a woman can take the lead. That shows a lot of maturity."

"I ain't never been the kind of man to squash a woman's strength. Every real man knows that a man is more physical, but a woman will always be more cerebral and mentally strong. Jehovah created us all equal. He gave us men the muscle, and you Queens the brains. We are flowing together as one, though. Who is this nigga?"

"I was wondering when you were going to get around to asking me that. Let's just say that he's very important in the game, and his opinions go a long way with deciding how far upward you reach before you are halted or snatched up by the Feds."

"What, fuck type of power he got?" Macho's mind began to race.

Angela laughed." A nice amount actually. "She stepped in front of him. When the time is right, he will be revealed. Until then, I've held up my end. It's time that you hold up yours." She slowly opened her robe and ran her hand along her stomach. Her see-through panties were stuffed into the slit of her pussy lips. They were fat and engorged.

"Bitch turn around, let me see that fat ass booty, too." He took a swallow from his bottle.

Angela got chills with how he was talking to her. She was a woman of extreme status and privilege. She wasn't accustomed to any man disrespecting her in the least bit. She turned in a circle in a tempting fashion.

Macho saw the way her ass was poked out and his dick started to rise immediately. It had been a few months since he and Lashawn had done anything and he was fiening for some pussy. He sat down his bottle. "Come here, bitch."

Angela walked to him and stood between his legs. "What you want lil' daddy?"

"Yo', you gotta be every bit of forty, right?"

She frowned. "Forty-two! Why is that important?" She started to become self-conscious. *Could he tell her age just by looking at her body? Did she need more surgery to preserve her youth?* Her insecurity began to take over.

Macho grabbed her by her panties and took a hold of her rounded ass. He squeezed the globes. "Yo', ever since I was a shorty, I done had mommy issues. I think older women fuckin' the game up." He leaned forward and sniffed her pussy lips. "You wanna be my mama for the night?"

Angela ran her tongue over her lips. "How can I do that?"

"Well—" Macho rubbed her pussy through the panties. "I wanna tear this grown pussy up and talk that shit in yo' ear. If you was my old girl I'd be fuckin' you every single day and we'd keep that shit between us. Ain't no way I could have yo' fine ass walking around our crib, and be able to keep my hands to myself. Look at how fat this pussy is." Macho yanked her panties to the side. "You ain't got no son?" He peeled apart her sex lips and licked up and down her crease.

"Mmm, yeah I do." She spaced her feet apart to give him better access.

Macho skipped two fingers into her and proceeded to run them in and out in slow motion digging deeper and deeper. "Has he ever got to see you dressed up like this with this fat ass pussy, and these ass cheeks hanging out of these panties the way they are?" He opened her lips and sucked on her clitoris.

"Nooooo, that's my son! Unnnnnn! Why would he get to see me like this?" She threw her head back imagining showing herself off to him.

Macho nipped at her clit and removed his mouth. He fingered her faster and faster. "Because when a nigga got a mama this fine, trust me, he thinks about it. But that's cool cause tonight you my mama. I'm yo' baby. You hear me?" He stabbed his fingers deep.

"Uhhhhhhh, yes baby! Yes, shit!" She squatted down while his fingers shot in and out of her. She imagined that it was her son Andre and came all over his fingers. "Uhhhhhh, fuck baby. Shit, my baby!"

Macho stood up and wiped his fingers on her chest. He picked her up and carried her to the big bed. He ripped her robe from her frame. "You finna give me some of this pussy mama. I can't take it anymore. You're too fine. I gotta see what this pussy feels like. He tore her negligée down the middle and ripped her panties away. Her thick thighs popped wide open. Her pussy was leaking with the sex lips fully engorged. She closed her eyes and imagined it was Andre overpowering her. The forbidden thought caused her to shiver. Macho got between her thighs and sucked on her neck. He bit into it. She moaned loudly and arched her back raising partway from the bed. Macho fumbled to get his dick out.

He kicked his shorts down and lined himself up. "You finna give me this mama!"

Chapter 5

"No!" Angela groaned. "It's not right, it's a sin." Her thick thighs cocked wide open and pussy juice leaked into her ass crack now.

"You my mafuckin' mama!" Macho slammed home and sunk deep into her pussy.

She moaned and dug her nails into his shoulder blades. He cocked back and plunged forward again, repeated the same process until he was biting into her neck and long stroking her at full speed. Her thick thighs jiggled and his spit ran down her neck. He sucked loudly feeling all over her with his eyes closed imagining that she really was his ol' girl. The forbidden side of him bubbled to the surface.

"Uhhh, mama, fuck this pussy good." He stroked harder and faster.

Bam! Bam! Bam! Bam!

Angela held her knees apart while Andre fucked her like he owned her pussy. She licked her lips and gushed when she felt his teeth bite into her neck again.

"Fuck me, baby. Fuck mama. Hit this pussy, unnhhh, you so deep!" she groaned.

She grabbed a hold of his shoulders and pulled him down to her. She licked the side of his face and wound up sucking on his ear lobe, flicking it with her tongue.

Macho moaned, he pushed her thick thighs to her breasts and bussed her pussy wide open. Her brown lips spread. He watched his dick go in and out of her gates. Her secretions leaked all around his pole and dripped off his balls that were crashing into her sex over and over. He panted, and stroked deeper and faster, pulling her to him once again.

Angela tried to break his hold, but it was of no use. She was trapped. No matter what she did she couldn't get away from him. Instead, she was forced to feel his thick penis running in and out of her. It felt as if his dick was getting longer and longer with each stroke.

She screamed at the top of her lungs and came hard. "Fuck me! Fuck me, baby. Awwww, my baby!"

Macho dipped into her ten more times before throwing her on her side. He grabbed her hips and slid back in, pulling her to him over and over again while he went deeper and deeper. "Pull them titties out, bitch! I wanna see 'em. Hurry up," he panted.

"Awww, fuck!" His dick ran in and out of her at full speed.

Angela felt like she was being stuffed to the max. She grabbed her left strap and pulled it off her shoulder. Her breasts popped out with the nipple heavily engorged.

Macho sucked it into his mouth and sped up once again. He licked all around it in a circular motion. He pulled it with his lips and hollered that he was cumming. Her fat booty crashed into his lap. He hurried to his knees and pushed her to her stomach. He fell on her back, long stroking her going as deep as he could.

"I'm finna cum, mama! I'm finna cum in this pussy. Tell me no! Tell me noooo, bitch!"

Angela spaced her thighs. "No! Stop! Uhhhhhh, shit stop!" She tooted her ass up just enough and felt him cumming deep inside her in large jets.

Macho grabbed ahold of her booty for leverage and plunged harder and harder while he spit his seed. He pulled his dick out and came all over her ass cheeks. He rubbed the head all in the mess, and opened her cheeks, rubbing her rosebud in a circular motion before he pushed his finger inside of her.

Angela was up on her elbows, she spread her knees again. "You wanna fuck mommy, right there, baby?"

Macho already had his tongue licking in a circular motion. He slid the digit deep into her ass and stood up on his knees. He pushed his nutty head inside of her back door and wasted no time fucking her ass like a savage. She was so thick. Her big booty crashed into his stomach again and again.

Angela threw her ass back into his lap once again imagining that it was Andre. *What if she actually had the guts to let him fuck her there,* she thought.

The imagery alone made her whimper as she saw his dick bottoming her out. She laid with her face sideways on the bed, twerking in his lap for twenty minutes until he came all over her lower back in big globs.

***

After their shower, Macho popped two Percs and chased it with a dirty Sprite. He sat on the edge of the bed while Angela laid on her back rubbing her pussy looking at him. She placed her right foot in his lap and fumbled with his dick. Her pretty toes looked gorgeous manipulating his tool. Macho laid back and allowed her to continue until his dick rose longer than he'd ever remembered seeing it.

Angela giggled. "You got quite the imagination, Macho. If I wasn't too careful, I would swear up and down that you and your mother actually got down before." She was fishing and hoping she hadn't overstepped the line.

Macho picked up her foot and sucked each toe one at a time. He looked to his left and could see directly between her thighs. Her bald pussy was fat. The lips were slightly parted because of their sex romp. Angela was a sexy ass older woman and she made him feel a way.

"Yo', so what if we did, that shit ain't ya bidness." He licked the length of her foot and sucked the toes again. "What size are you?"

"Six, and I didn't mean any disrespect. I was just making an observation." She gave him her other foot.

Macho sucked the toes and lowered them to his dick. There was something about pretty, small feet all over his piece that drove him crazy. He was fascinated by the mature feminine body. "Yo', it doesn't matter how me and my moms really living. All I can say is that if you were my old girl I'd be fuckin' you every day, and I wouldn't give a fuck what nobody says. Ain't nothin' sexier than an older woman. Young hoez gotta get to the throne that y'all are already sitting on. I even like these, right here."

He rubbed over her stretch marks that lightly decorated her stomach. "When I was just a lil' boy, my mother told me these were a woman's badge of honor. These right here were Jehovah's way of letting men know that a woman was capable of doing something that a man could never do. She was able to give life. Yo', that's bananas." He leaned over and licked her stomach tracing the marks, then rubbing his face over them.

Angela placed her fingers in his dreads and rubbed the side of his face. "Yeah, if you were my baby I think you'd make me go. I'd probably hate myself after the first time, but after that, I'd be wit' it on a regular basis. It helps that you are so fuckin' sexy to me. I love your dark skin, it makes your brown eyes pop."

Macho nodded. "Chocolate is the deal, everybody knows that. He licked her stomach and placed his nose in her belly button, he scooted down and kissed her pussy. "I woulda been all over you every time my pops turned his back. You sexy as fuck."

Angela giggled. "I'm glad you think so. Most men are running and chasing behind those young girls. They don't even pay vets like me any attention outside of my status. They think the younger the pussy the better."

"Fuck them, I'm vet crazy." He tongue kissed the inside of her slit for ten minutes.

Angela bucked and shoved his face into her gap and came rotating her hips. She fell back onto the bed breathing hard. Her nipples were so hard that they hurt. "I gotta keep you close, Macho. There is something about you that drives me crazy." She sat up on her elbows. "Now get up here and I'm going to explain to you how we are about to take over Philly."

***

It was a wet and rainy Thursday night when Burleigh pulled his blue Hummer up in front of one of the many trap houses that Macho ran. He had three foreign cars behind him filled with armed killers. He hopped out of his Hummer after pulling behind Macho's Benz and waited until one of his shooters knocked on the trap house's door. The shooter hustled down the steps and stood with his Mach-11 at the ready.

Macho was in the house overseeing three bricks of the Rebirth being bust down for distribution. When he heard the knock on the door he hopped up and cocked his Glock 40. "Yo', see who the fuck that is, kid."

One of his Cutthroat goddesses stuck her face in the window and spotted Burleigh right away. Her eyes got big when she saw how many people were with him. "Say, Dunn, that's Burleigh, Pooh's brother outside. Kid got like fifty people wit' him and they are all armed. What you wanna do?" She kneeled and picked up a Mach-90.

"*Burleigh?* I thought that fuck nigga got indicted?" Macho backed down the hallway headed toward the back door. "Yo', wait for my command. He got on his cell and called for his hittas to block off the strip. He ordered them to make haste to his location. He told them to wait for his go ahead before they splashed anything. As soon as he hung up the phone there was a knock on the door. Macho jumped, he cursed and headed toward the front of the trap. "Yo', pack my dope up bitch, and go put it in the safe. Lock my shit and your job is to protect it with your life. You hear me blood?"

"Loud and clear, Slime. I'm on it." She proceeded to follow his order.

Macho peeked out the window again. He saw Burleigh standing on the porch at the same time Preston pulled up in his black Jaguar. He hopped out of it with Kayley on side of him, both were armed with assault rifles, and had mugs on their faces. Preston stepped into Burleigh's face.

This prompted Macho to open the front door. "Yo', fuck you want wit' the God, son?"

"This Cutthroat hood right here, Slime. Ain't nothing blue over this way that stays that way for long," Preston hissed looking into Burleigh's eyes.

Burleigh was five-feet-eight, heavyset with long nappy dreadlocks. He was light-skinned and known for being a silent killer, and drug lord. He smiled at Preston. "Nigga, I ain't been locked up but a few months fighting my case. I know you ain't turned into a cold-blooded killer that fast, knock it off," he said this dismissing him.

Kayley jumped Preston out of the way. "Yeah, blood, well, if he ain't I am." She upped her Mach and aimed it at his face. "Now what?"

Burleigh's crew upped their guns and aimed them at Kayley and the trap house as a whole. Members of the Cutthroat mafia began pulling up on location hopping out of their cars with big guns, and even grenades. They wore red rags over their faces or black ski masks ignoring the rain. Before it was all said and done the block was packed with a hundred and twenty Cutthroat killas and only twenty of Burleigh's Payroll boys.

Burleigh mugged Kayley. "Yo', somebody check this bitch before she starts a war. I'm only over here to find out what happened to my little brother. I ain't trying to bring no noise unless I have to."

"Yo', who you callin' a bitch, blood?" Preston nudged Kayley to the side.

"Yeah, nigga, don't disrespect our goddesses. They covered under the blood of Cutthroat," Macho let it be known.

"I don't give a fuck about none of that. Check this bitch or we finna send this mafucka to the moon, word up," Burleigh snapped. He was used to being in power. He refused to be disrespected by anybody, especially a female. "What happened to Pooh?"

"Yo', son, you gon' keep ya mouth dirty, huh? Yeah, a'ight then. Fuck you then. Get 'em, baby girl." Preston stepped back.

Kayley stepped forward. "Gang gang, fuck nigga." She upped her Mach and shredded his face all along the side of the door. He dropped, she stood over him and kept pulling the trigger bucking him down.

Preston smiled and snatched her up pulling her into the trap just as a bunch of shots rang out in their direction. "Fuck!"

Kayley landed on her back. She saw Macho back up with his Glock .40. She jumped up and ran to the back of the house, and out the back door as rapid-fire sounded. She stood on the side of the gangway finger fucking her gun-running at the Payroll killas that were already under attack by the Cutthroat hittas. She yearned for more bloodshed. She craved it. She felt like the more men she was able to annihilate the stronger she would feel as a woman.

Her choppa jumped in her hands, spitting bullet after bullet out of it. The shells clinked on the pavement and rolled with smoke coming off them. When Kayley made it to the front of the trap house most of the Payroll boys were laid out in the street with bullet wounds all over them. They struggled to maintain their lives, while the other ones retreated like cowards. There were a few of the Cutthroat hittas laid out bleeding as well. Kayley walked from body to body turning its lights out. When there were no more people kicking and hanging on to the edge of death, she grabbed Preston, and they sped away from the scene after rolling over more than one dead body.

Chapter 6

"A'ight now, Preston. I'm nervous as hell for you to meet my mother. Sometimes she can be a bit extra, but just know that she means well, and she has a big heart. So, try your best to be smooth. As far as my sister, Kim-Kim goes she means well also. Keep in mind I ain't seen my family in months and that I really need this so I can feel like my old self again. Got it?" she said this eyeing, Preston suspiciously before she looked up at her mother's three-story brick home.

"Yo', you talking to the kid like he doesn't know how to behave himself. It's good Goddess. I know you need for me to hold you down, and I got you." He leaned over and kissed her cheek.

Kayley smiled. "Thanks, daddy. You ready to do this?" She tried to build up her nerves.

"Yeah, let's make it happen." Before they could get out of the rented red Ferrari, the front door opened.

"Aw shit, here we go," Kayley uttered.

Kim-Kim appeared on the porch with a short, figure-fitting, Fendi skirt dress on that made her natural curves look delectable. She was bare feet just like a real country girl. She was five-feet-five, caramel-skinned, with brown eyes, and the body of a goddess. Her hair was curly and shoulder length. She nearly twisted her ankle to get to the car so she could hug her little sister.

When she got to the passenger's side, she knocked on the window. "Stop playin' and get yo' butt out here, Kayley. I can't believe this girl rolling in a Ferrari. I thought these were illegal in Houston."

Kayley stepped out of the car and slid her Chanel frames onto her face. It was a hundred and five degrees out and with the humidity, it felt like it was every bit of a hundred and twenty. She began to sweat as soon as she stepped out of the air-conditioned Ferrari.

Kim-Kim hugged Kayley tight. "Girl, I ain't seen yo' ass in forever. I can't even believe you're really here." She hugged her tighter with her eyes closed. She opened them just as Preston stood up and slid his Gucci shades on his face. His deep waves glistened in the sunlight. He was fitted from head to toe in Gucci, even his gold Gucci belt offset his loafers. "Damn, who is he?" Kim-Kim stepped back and started to choose right away.

Kayley mugged her. "That's my baby daddy. He would've been if I hadn't lost the baby. I mean you know what I'm saying. His name is Preston."

Kim-Kim walked around Kayley and held her hand out, giving it to Preston. "Well, well, well, Preston, nice to meet you. My sister ain't tell me much about you but that ain't necessarily a bad thing."

Preston moved her hand and hugged her body to his. She yelped having been caught off guard. He noted right away that she was thick and slightly bow-legged.

He held her for a second and kissed her cheek. "Nice to meet you, Shorty."

Kim-Kim shuddered and blushed. "It's nice to meet you too." She could feel his muscles wrapped around her and it caused her to feel a way. She wisely eased out of his embrace with Kayley mugging her like crazy. She stepped in front of her sister. "How was your flight? Are they still trying to figure the whole social distancing thing out?"

Kayley nodded. "Yeah, it's one thing after another with those people, I'll be glad when they get that goofy out of the white house. Where is mama?"

Kim-Kim lit up. "She's inside and she can't wait to see you, come on." She took a hold of her sister's hand and led her upstairs and into the house with Preston following close behind.

When they got inside, Jackie was running back and forth from the oven to the set table. She had so much food on the top of it that it was hard for her to find a place to set anything else. She heard them come in and wiped her hands on her apron.

"Is that my baby?" she screeched.

She looked just like a slightly older version of Kayley. She was beautiful. She rushed to her daughter and wrapped her arms around her.

Kayley began to cry right away. "Mama, I missed you so bad. I've been wanting to come home, but I've just been so busy. And then this whole pandemic doesn't know what it wanna do. One minute it's getting weaker, and the next it's stronger. It's ridiculous." She hugged her tighter.

Jackie rubbed her back, she had tears in her eyes as well. After they hugged for a spell, she stepped back and held her daughter's face in her small hands. "Girl, you look like you're losing weight. You been eating anything?"

Kayley shook her head. "Not really, I ain't had an appetite. But it sure smells good in here."

Jackie kissed her. "Southern and Cajun Style everything. I'ma make sure I send you back to Baltimore with some meat on yo' bones."

"Yo', my jewel got hella meat on her. She's perfect," Preston said, smiling.

"Oh, is that right, and just who might you be?" Jackie walked up to him.

Preston took hold of her hand and kissed the back of it. "I'm going to be your son in law. I bought you this. I didn't know your favorite flavor, so I just grabbed pink lemonade."

Jackie took the jewelry box and opened it to reveal a pair of three-carat pink lemonade diamond earrings. They twinkled in the kitchen. She took a deep breath and exhaled slowly. "Well, you sure know how to make an entrance don't you?" She smiled at him and found him handsome. *Good for Kayley,* she thought.

"My baby was telling me how much you meant to her, so I had to come correct. I hope you like them." Preston eyed, Kayley. She nodded at him with approval.

"I love them, Pink lemonade just happens to be my favorite." She closed her eyes and batted them at him playfully.

"My sister must don't mess with me because you ain't get me nothing." Kim-Kim crossed her arms displeased.

"Yeah, right, I just had to make sure the queen of the throne was taken care of first. I got you straight ice, no flavor." He handed her a rectangular box.

Kim-Kim opened it to reveal a diamond tennis bracelet dripping in clarity. Her eyes lit up, and her middle got moist. She fidgeted on her bare feet and took the bracelet out of the box. "Wow, this is beautiful. You showing out." She hugged him again.

Preston laughed. "You're welcome."

"A'ight, now, that we have the gifts squared away it's time to eat and get full. Kayley, I want you to catch us up on your entire wellbeing out there in Baltimore, and we'll get you caught up with our soap operas out dis way. Sound like a plan?" Jackie slid her arm around her daughter's lower back.

Kayley smiled. "It sure does. Let's eat."

***

"I'm glad to see that you hit it off with my people, I ain't gon' even lie. I was a little worried about that." Kayley dropped her bra and panties and slipped into a short black nightgown. She sat on the bed and took her earrings off.

Preston pulled off his shirt, he was heavily tatted. "Yo', diamonds are a girl's best friend. I don't give a fuck what girl it is, word up." He dropped his shorts and folded them up. He walked across the room in his Gucci boxers.

"Yeah, well, you most definitely proved that you're my man. I appreciate you for holding me down. That means a lot." She climbed under the covers and got comfortable. Her eyes strained to remain open.

Preston eyed her from across the room. "I guess hitting that pussy under your mother's roof would be foul, huh?" He sat on the bed and rubbed the covers that were sunk between her thighs. It felt hot to his touch.

Kayley kept her thighs open for him. "I gotta get a few hours of sleep and then we can do whatever. I'll give you some." She winked at him. "You feel like fuckin'?"

He stood up and pulled down his boxers. "Hell yeah, look at this mafucka." His piece was at half mass and already thick as her wrist.

She laughed and pulled it to her. She sucked the head into her mouth, bobbing up and down for five minutes. She popped it out and ran it all over her face. "When I wake up, I got you, boo. I just need like three hours, shit, even two would be cool."

"Yo', I'm wide awake. What am I supposed to do, watch you sleep?"

She shook her head. "Go see if they're up. Like I said, all I need is a few hours. Come back then." She pulled the sheets over her head. "Wake me up at one."

Preston threw back on his shorts and beater. He turned off the lamp and closed the guest room door behind him disgruntled. He eased into the hallway and looked down it to see that the living room light was on. He made his way there crossing,

Jackie's bedroom door. He heard *Mary J. Blige* coming from it. He laughed and thought about Lashawn, Mary J. Blige was her favorite singer. When he stepped into the living room, Kim-Kim was sitting in the white leather loveseat.

She crossed her thick caramel thighs and looked up at him. "What, my sister getting on your nerves?"

Preston slipped on to the couch across from her. He shook his head. "N'all, she's just tired, I'm restless. What's good wit' you, though?"

She picked up the remote control. "Nothin', I was 'bout to watch *A Bronx Tale* movie. But I already know boys don't like sappy stuff like that so you can watch whatever you wanna watch since you the guest. She sat up, spread her thighs, and leaned her arm across the glass table to hand him the remote.

From his vantage point, Preston could see all up her gown. It was almost around her waist. She saw him looking and closed her thighs embarrassed. "Here you go."

Preston took the remote and turned the big screen to Sports Center. "I gotta see what the King doing."

"Aw, you like LeBron too, huh?"

"He and his son, ain't nobody better. You fuck wit' the homies?" He eyed her legs again.

She followed his eyes and nodded. "Yeah, always have. Ever since he played in Cleveland the first time." She slightly opened her thighs. "I guess you really took heed when I said that since you're the guest you can watch anythang you want? Cause you're definitely trying to see this." She slowly eased up her gown and opened her knees. "I know it's fat ain't it. Whenever you ain't supposed to have something it always looks so good." She ran her finger up the middle of her slit. "I ain't never fucked wit' a baller before. My sister tends to always get those boys that got that paper. Seems like ever since that George Floyd stuff, ain't nothing but bums running around Houston protecting instead of working. Kinda wish I had myself a man that roll Ferraris." She stepped on her toes and really bussed her pussy wide open.

Preston's piece throbbed so much he had to reach inside his shorts and adjust it. He squeezed it for a second then released it. "Damn, Shorty, you better close them thighs before you get a mafucka in trouble."

Kim-Kim sunk a finger into herself and pulled it out. She sucked her juices off it and savored her taste. "Ain't nothing wrong wit' looking long as you don't touch." She placed her right foot on the couch and opened her brown lips for him to look inside of her pink. She tweaked her clit and whimpered. "Fuck, you see that daddy?"

Preston hopped up. "Yo', you thick as fuck. That's how you southern hoez coming?"

"We sho' is. Now what you talking 'bout?" She licked her juicy lips. "I'm showing you mine. Can I see yours?" She sunk two fingers deep into her pussy and groaned.

Preston felt his knees go weak. He took a step toward her with his fingers on the button of his shorts. As soon as he started to unbutton them he heard Jackie's door open and the Mary J. Blige song got louder.

Jackie stepped out into the hallway nodding her head to her music with a big smile on her face. She wore a short robe that was loosely tied. In her right finger was a freshly rolled joint that she'd already taken five puffs off of. She was feeling the effects. She stepped into the living room and eyed Preston.

She looked him up and down hungrily. "Say, baby, you ever danced to Mary J. Blige before?" She stepped in front of him and slid her left arm around his waist.

Kim-Kim pulled her gown down and walked into the kitchen. She felt hot and bothered and a bit guilty for coming on to her sister's man the way that she had. "Mama, leave that boy alone before Kayley comes in here and goes berserk. You already know how she is about her dudes." Kim-Kim was thinking she should've taken her own advice.

"Girl just shut up. You're always the party pooper. Now if I wanna dance with my son-in-law to be, then I'ma do just that. Long as he ain't saying that he got a problem with me being all up on him, it ain't fa you to bump yo' gums. Butt out." She rolled her eyes at her daughter, before looking up to Preston. "What do you say, baby? You wanna dance wit' yo' mama-in-law to be?" She slipped her hands around his neck, then slowly trailed them down his chest and the bit of gut that he had all while looking him seductively in the eyes.

"Hell yeah, I'll dance wit' you, Jackie. Ain't nothing wrong wit' grooving wit' a seasoned dime. Word up, you killing that robe cutie," Preston said this all while eyeing the slope of her breasts.

They were mostly visible in the loose robe. He already knew he was going to maneuver her to make sure that he was able to catch a glimpse of what she had to offer. Jackie was sexy to him, and her pheromones were sending him up the wall.

Jackie stepped forward and placed her face in the crux of his neck. "One thang 'bout us country girls is that we keep our family real close-knit. Find a good man and sometimes he may get just a bit of affection from the whole house. Doesn't matter who he is that's all I reckon." She kissed his neck softly. "I can see the print of your log in those lil' shorts. Boy, I been looking at it all day." She slipped her hand between them and grabbed his piece.

Preston didn't say a word. Instead, he wanted to see where she was going to take things. He closed the distance between them and began to groove with her. From over his shoulder, he spotted Kim-Kim in the kitchen. She pulled her shoulder straps down and flashed him her pretty brown breasts. While he watched her, she tweaked her pacifier sized nipples and pulled up her gown to show him her pussy once again. The plump lips were puffy and heavily engorged.

Preston's dick throbbed. He groaned when Jackie unbuttoned his shorts and slipped her hand into his boxers.

She stroked his dick and sucked his neck. "You like that city boy?"

He groaned, "Yo', you wilding."

The guest bedroom door opened, Kayley staggered into the hallway and went right into the bathroom. She slammed the door, before pulling up the toilet seat and sitting down, with her eyes closed she began to pee.

Jackie licked Preston's lips. "Boy, if you don't leave this living room, me and Kim-Kim gon' eat yo' ass alive. We don't play when it comes to pipes like these." She squeezed his dick harder. "We Southern girls. Feel this." She took his hand and placed it under her robe. His fingers guided over her trim bush. The lips were meaty and wet. Her scent drifted to his nose and made his piece jump.

"Mmm, yo' I'm 'bout what y'all 'bout." Preston heard the toilet flush.

Jackie pushed him away and disappeared into her room. Kim-Kim opened the refrigerator door and acted like she was looking for something to eat when Kayley walked into the living room. Preston's dick was so hard that he had to sit down.

Kayley stepped in front of him. "Yo', you coming to bed, kid?" She looked into the kitchen and spotted Kim-Kim, then she looked back at Preston.

"Yeah, shorty, here I come. I'll meet you there." Preston tried to think about every nigga that he'd ever slumped so his piece could go down. He thought about fighting, shoot outs, heroin addicts, funerals, slowly his piece began to weaken.

Kayley eyed Kim-Kim again. "Yeah, a'ight den. Fuck she in there doing wit' that lil' ass gown on?"

Kim-Kim stood up with her big nipples visible. "I was finna make yo' nigga some leftovers but since y'all finna go to sleep, shit I am, too. Good night." She avoided eye contact with Kayley, and walked off, into her bedroom.

Preston jumped up. "Well, that's that. Come on, I'm finna wear that ass out." He grabbed her hand and pulled her into their guest bedroom, where Kayley stiffed him and made him hold her all night.

Chapter 7

It was a bright and sunny day when Preston lifted the Lamborghini doors of his rented Ferrari for Kim-Kim to get into. She slid into the passenger's seat and looked around as if she was getting into a spaceship. "Wow, Preston, I ain't never been inside some shit like this before. You must got that stupid dough." She sat back and pulled her seat belt across her perky chest.

Preston closed the door as gentleman like as he could. He walked across the back of the Ferrari and slid into the driver's seat. "Yo' this shit light work. This mafucka just rented. I ain't feel like rolling through Houston like a bum. Plus, yo' sister gotta ride in style. That's just how that shit gotta go." He pulled down the door, and started the ignition, then pulled from in front of the house. He turned on Tee Grizzley's new album and let it play. He fucked wit' Tee Grizzley the long way.

"So, I'm saying, if we going out, does that just mean you finna spend some money on me? I ain't really got too many things and it seems like you got a whole lot, Playboy." She crossed her thighs. "You be spoiling Kayley and all that jazz."

Preston side-eyed her legs. She was wearing a knock off pink Prada skirt over the fake Prada halter top. Her sandals were cheap, too. Preston shook his head at her poor-quality material. "Yo', you fine as a muthafucka, shorty. Why ain't no nigga getting you together the way he supposed to be?"

She shrugged her shoulders. "These boys are cheap in the south. Most times it be us women spending money on them. Can't say I can think of one right man that spent a bit of cash on his old lady. Kayley done struck a pot of gold, that's what she done did." She looked Preston over. "'Sides, I may be older but we got different daddies and all and hers brought her out there to the East coast a whole lot. Mine is an old farmer. Slow as a snail in traffic. All I know is the South, and we ain't much faster than a red light chile' I tell you." She licked her juicy lips. "You think I'ma bum, huh?"

Preston nodded. "Yeah, shorty."

She popped his thigh with her hand. "Dang mane, you weren't 'pose to agree wit' me. You shoulda had a mind to tell me what I wanted to hear for a spell. Just rude as a man farting at the dinner table." She mugged him.

Preston laughed. "Yo', I'm serious, but I'm just fuckin' wit you, too." He rubbed her thigh. "How you get so damn thick?"

She shrugged her shoulders. "Don't know. I guess it runs in my genes. You saw my mother. She is just as thick and so is Kayley. Of course, she got a lot of her father's side of the genes wit' all of their salad eating and thangs. I gotta have some meat. If I wanted to eat grass I'd dine with lawnmowers."

Preston laughed again. "Yo', lil' ass sho got a way wit' words."

"I speak 'em as I think 'em." She turned toward him. "You think I look a lil' better than, Kayley?"

"What, why would you ask me something like that?"

"I see the way you looking at me is all. Ain't seen you stare at her so intently. Just wondering if you saw somethin' you liked a bit more? No need to get the grumbles. Plus, I know she is gorgeous. I'm so sick of living in her chocolate shadow, though. One of these days I'ma get out of the house and become something great. I can sang better than Ariana Grande', do it in church all the time, just too shy outside of it, and ain't got the duckies for a studio session."

"Yo', you got some pipes on you?"

She leaned into his lap. "Wouldn't you like to know?" Her lip gloss shimmered.

Preston cruised for a moment riding through the streets of Houston and wasn't impressed with the slums and the things that he saw. Everybody was wearing Coronavirus masks, and gloves for the most part. The streets looked run down, and heavily littered. There were murals of George Floyd and Breonna Taylor on a lot of the walls. He crossed himself with the crucifix and said a silent prayer for the two fallen angels.

"Yo', goddess I'll tell you what. You wanna go shopping and all that shit, right?"

She nodded. "Yeah, I do, but my money got jokes right now."

"Yo', fuck yo' chips cutie, check dis out. You saying you got pipes and all that right?"

She began to undo his Ferragamo belt. "I already know where this is going."

He popped her hand. "Chill out and get ya mind out of the gutter. Now listen, all you gotta do to get some gear is blow me away."

She was confused as she licked her lips. "But that's what I was getting ready to do." She gripped his dick through his pants.

He shook his head. "Nall bitch, I'm talking about singing. I want you to hit a song for me. If you can really sing, not only will I take you shopping, but I'll book you a few studio sessions. Deal or no deal?"

Kim-Kim closed her eyes. She licked her juicy lips and began to blow *At Last* by *Etta James*. She blew it so beautifully that Preston got chills. Then she blew three songs off Arianna Grandès' album flawlessly.

Preston pulled the car to the side of the road and gave her a round of applause. "Yo', hand to God you is a beast. Point me to the nearest studio, we about to get you right this moment."

***

It was one o'clock in the morning when Lashawn rushed into the house and closed the door behind her. She stopped in the living room of her apartment and stripped her coat off. She pulled the heroin out of her inner pocket and slid her hand under the couch to grab her work. She sat crossed legged, and in a matter of minutes had her dope fixed up the way that she needed it to be. She tied the rope around her arm and waited until a vein popped up before she slid the syringe into it and injected the Rebirth heroin. She moaned out loud. Her eyes rolled into the back of her head. She slowly sprawled out on the floor with a smile on her face. Images of Lashonda came across her mind. She saw birthday parties for her little girl. She saw her first day of school. She felt as if she could still hear her pretty voice calling to her. She closed her eyes, as tears sailed down her cheeks.

"It's not fair! It's just not fair."

***

Macho tossed and turned in his bed with his eyes squeezed shut. He kicked the covers off him and felt like he couldn't breathe. He sat up and let out a gust of air. He held his throat and jumped out of the bed drenched in sweat. He fell to his knees trying to come to grips with reality and the fact that he was no longer dreaming. Lashonda had once again plagued his subconscious. She begged him for the reason he killed her. She asked him didn't he love her. She cried and told him to take her to her mommy before she began to choke him, and that's when he woke up.

He stood up and wiped his face. He walked over to his dresser and snorted two lines of Percocets. He tilted his head back with his nostrils pinched. A slow opiate drip slid down to the back of his throat. He swallowed and took a step back. He staggered and looked toward the ceiling of the room.

"I'm sorry, Lashonda. You know I would never hurt you, baby. You were as much my daughter as you were his. I was crazy about you. I didn't know you were with him. If I had I woulda never pulled the trigger." Tears ran down his face.

He lowered his head and stepped back up to the platter of narcotics tooting over and over until the inside of his nose became raw and the pain and remorse deep within his heart began to dissipate.

Ghost

Chapter 8

The next day Macho flew above Philadelphia inside a black Chopper with Angela Simms sitting beside him deepthroating his dick. She moaned around his piece until the pilot announced that they were now above Kensington Park around North Philly. She picked her head up out of his lap, and wiped her mouth, then applied her red MAC lipstick.

"Okay, baby, we're here. You see that area just below us? That is what we call North Philly. It is the deadliest and the most drug-infested area of the entire city of brotherly love. The savages that dwell there are cutthroat, cold-hearted, and will do anything for a blue face hundred-dollar bill. Not only do you have to watch those that are jackers. You also have to watch those that we will be forced to go into business with. Philly is like Baltimore on steroids." She smiled. "But on the contrary, with a product like the Rebirth that you have, and the way you have your operations, and your troops set up. I am most certain that not only will you be able to infiltrate the drug trade here, but with the right moves, you may even be able to master and conquer it."

Macho mugged the scene below. As far as he could tell it simply looked like a bunch of houses and apartment buildings that were stuck together. It reminded him of Baltimore, both cities' physical makeups were identical. "Yo', I'm closing in on five hundred thousand dollars a day in B-more. Fuck I stand to make out dis way?"

Angela pointed toward Kensington Park. "You play yo' cards right. You can double that chump change here. That means if you keep your operations going the way that you have them in Baltimore, you will be able to pull one point five million every single day. That's crazy money."

"Not really when you are forced to feed so many people. While the number sounds good it really isn't that much. Since I'm planning on taking over this bitch, that means I gotta bring a bunch of troops from Baltimore and even snatch up a few out here that know the ropes. Yo', your army ain't shit if they ain't loyal, deep, and eating at a buffet. Niggas will snuff you and put you on the menu quick. I gotta touch bases with a few of the young savages and find out which one of the clan got a connection to some bloodthirsty killas out here in Philly. Street politics is everything, straight up."

Angela loved when Macho spoke that drug lord, kingpin talk. It made her pussy wet. Even though she was a woman of privilege it still made her feel a way about being connected to the streets through a killer like Macho.

"I'ma do my part too, baby. There is nothing that goes on in the hood that can't be bought with the right amount of money. I'ma buy you an army."

"N'all Shorty, step yo' ass back before I choke the fuck out of you. I don't need you doing shit for me when it comes to the trenches. I got this, and a mafucka held his own. Second, to that, you need to finish hitting the kid off anyway. You using up too much of your word count." He pushed her face into his lap and felt her inhale his dick. "Yo', son, spin around North Philly a few more times so I can get this mafucka in my soul," he hollered this to the pilot.

"Will do, sir."

Macho wrapped his fingers into Angela's hair. "Eat the don, I got a whole lot of thinking to do."

***

Lashawn opened her eyes and ran her hand across her face. She had a splitting headache, her mouth was dry, and her stomach felt like it was in knots. She came to a sit and scooted backward until her back was against the wall in her living room. She winced in pain with her eyes closed.

"Damn, sugar, 'bout time you woke yo' ass up. I was 'bout to do this fix without you," George said sitting on the couch.

Lashawn bucked her eyes wide open. "George, what the hell are you doing in my house?" she snapped and stood up disoriented. She felt dizzy and dope sick. Her stomach was queasy.

"Girl, after you done shot up all the dope I hustled for all yesterday. You gon' play the fool?" He smacked his lips. "Knock it off." He laughed and set up their works. He filled her syringe first. "Huh, you need to wake up."

Lashawn ran her fingers through her hair. She closed her eyes and reopened them. "Wait a minute, are you saying that I invited you into my home?"

George licked his lips. "Invited me to a lot more than that if you get my drift. Drank up my wine and then I got to see just how fine you was under that damn thang right there." He pointed at her.

Lashawn looked down and for the first time saw that she was only in a long tee-shirt that stopped just above her knees. She was naked underneath. She spotted the empty bottle of wine on the table and became sick to her stomach even more. "George, tell me that we ain't slept together, please. Please tell me that you ain't went inside of my body."

"Nope, I don't feel like using my first sin of the day up on yo' ass. Hell yeah, I hit that pussy girl. Fucked the shit out of you and got my money's worth. Sho' nuff did, too." He laughed. "You a freak too when you get that dope and liquor in you. Let me play wit' yo' booty and all that. Macho's lucky. Damn, sho' is. Now shoot up. We gon' buss this wine down next. I need me some more of that big body, wit' yo' thick ass."

"No, no, no, George. You're Macho's brother. Why would you do somethin' like this when you know he and I are together?"

George mugged her. "Girl is you stupid. How y'all together when you gotta buy dope off the street that Macho runs? He ain't thinking 'bout you. He got himself a new girl. She all high and mighty from New York and stuff. She got a helicopter and a whole bunch of money. I saw her on one of those talk shows. Wake up." He snapped his fingers. "Take that dope and let's get it on Marvin Gaye style." He cheesed and began to tie a belt around his arm.

Heroin pains shot all over Lashawn's body. She fell to her knees. "Wrap me up, please."

George sighed, and rushed over to tie a belt around, Lashawn's arm. When a vein appeared, she injected herself with the heroin and opened her mouth as if she was having the best orgasm of her life. She drew up her blood and pushed it back into her system, before pulling the needle out and licking her injection site. She moaned and fell back against the wall with her eyes low. George handed her the bottle of cheap wine already opened. She took it and downed half of it. He slipped next to her and began to feel all over her breasts.

***

Macho counted five hundred thousand dollars in cash before he stacked it strategically in his safe. Inside the room that he was sitting in were eight butt, naked females, from his Cut-throat Mafia. In front of them were money machines and piles of cash. Behind each of them stood an armed female guard that had been given orders to blow their heads off if anything looked fishy. Macho had two cameras in the room that he would often watch the footage of when he felt he needed to. He was high as a kite and had tooted more than one pill.

He kept imagining the sights of Philly. He couldn't wait to handle his business in a new location. Angela had told him that he could make up to one-point-five million dollars a day in the city alone. For him that was motivation. His profits in Baltimore had increased to seven hundred thousand a day before he had to pay his workers, his plug, his security, and before he greased as many palms as necessary.

After it was all said and done his take home was a little more than a hundred thousand. The game was cold and relentless, and it never gave a true hustler enough room to breathe. Macho accepted that fact, and it didn't bother him. He wanted to be a king. He yearned to be the number one drug lord in the game, and he didn't care what he had to do to reach that status.

After getting back to Baltimore the next day he turned up. He made his Rebirth bags fatter and lowered the prices by five dollars a bag. He stopped the sale of weight and only sold dimes and twenties. He focused solely on the users and cut off the other dope boys that were aligned with but not under his crew. He knew that if he honed on the dope addict side of the selling that his profits would increase tenfold, but that the jealousy meter would go high when it came to other hustlers. Macho didn't care. He upped his security and moved forward with his thought pattern. His goal was to make the entire city of Baltimore dependent upon the Cutthroat Mafia.

***

It was three in the morning, one hot and humid Thursday when Macho knocked on Lashawn's door. She opened it with her hair all over the place, smelling like she hadn't showered in nearly a month. He ignored the urge to want to pinch his nose. She wore a heavily stained white tee shirt and nothing else. When she saw him, she opened the door and walked away from it.

Macho nodded at three of his shooters, and they posted up on Lashawn's porch. Two more loaded on the side of her house, and two in the back. He had two patrol cars that spun the block over and over. He stepped into her place and now he pinched his nose. It smelled horrible. There were eight dope addicts laid out on the floor. Three of them were snoring so loud he didn't know how they didn't wake themselves up. He frowned and followed Lashawn into the kitchen where she was drinking out of the sink with two dirty hands.

He grabbed her by the hair. "Fuck is going on wit' you?"

She knocked his hand away from her hair and pushed him. "Get yo' fuckin' hands off me, Macho. I ain't yo' property." She stepped backward on a big brown roach that had an egg hanging out of its ass. She smashed it and didn't seem to notice. All around the kitchen roaches roamed freely. The sink was full of dirty dishes, and the floor had been tracked with mud.

Macho stood mugging her. "Yo', Shawn, you got a whole living room full of junkies in that bitch, man. You either serving them or you fuckin' wit 'em on some kicking it shit. If that's the case, why the fuck would you be kicking it wit' a bunch of hypes?"

"Macho, it ain't none of yo' bidness. I heard you got yo' self a real bad bitch now. You done gave up on me. You gave up and you left me to fend for myself! How could you?" She was pissed.

Macho grabbed a hold of her shoulders. "I ain't gave up on shit. If I gave up why would I be standing here, right now?"

Lashawn looked into his eyes at the same time a serious migraine quaked its way through her head. The heroin was calling her. "Macho, I don't have time for this right now. My head is hurting. I am still going through it and trying to seek closure within myself when it comes to the death of Lashonda. You ain't been here for me, and neither has, Preston. Y'all are out there living your lives to the best of your abilities and I chose to do the same thing. Now, what did you come over here for?"

"I missed you, baby. I've been thinking about you every single day. You are the one that said you needed space. I thought that by granting it to you, you would be able to restore yourself. I've been in your DMs every day, though. Why you ain't tell me you needed more?"

"What?" Lashawn glared at him. "I lost my little girl. You know how much she meant to me. How dare you ask me such a stupid question, Macho? God, sometimes you can seem so oblivious." She knocked his hands off her.

Macho grabbed her and slammed her against the wall. A roach fell off it and wound up on its back kicking its legs until it flipped over and scurried away. Macho held up her right arm. He spotted the track marks. "Fa real, Lashawn? You using that bullshit?"

Lashawn flared her nostrils and avoided his eyes. "I don't want to talk about it, Macho. You need to leave my house right now. Go on and live your life. Don't worry about me no more."

Macho lowered his eyes. "Yo', you think I give a fuck about you giving me an order? Especially if it's one that I don't plan on following. Man, fuck that. You about to pack yo' shit and enroll in rehab, right now. I ain't about to lose you to this drug shit. I love you way too much for that. So, come on." He pushed her toward her bedroom.

Lashawn jerked away from him. "Macho, I'm a grown-ass woman. You can't keep telling me what to do all the time."

"You my mafuckin' woman. I'd splash yo' ass before I let you fall like this. Now take yo' ass in there and get dressed. We leaving in ten minutes." He pushed her into the room, she fell on the bed. Macho cocked his .45 and headed into the living room. "Yo! You bitch ass geekers! Get the fuck up and out of my bitch's crib. Wake the fuck. This is your last warning!" He tapped the trigger of his gun and emitted a red beam from the laser on top of the gun.

One by one the addicts began taking their coats off their heads. They got up and rushed toward the exit as Macho mugging them. When all but one had left Macho walked over and kicked the last addict's dirty shoes. "Say, homic, get yo' punk ass up and out of my bitch crib. This yo' last warning."

George sat up and dropped his dirty Starter jacket. He locked eyes with Macho and stood up. He lowered his head. "What's up lil' bro? How you living, baby?" He inched toward the door.

Macho slid over and blocked his path. He held his gun straight out and pressed the barrel to his forehead and cocked the hammer. "Yo', on gang, bitch nigga you betta give me the best reason you can come up with for why you're over my Shorty's crib. You got three seconds."

"Shit." George threw his hands up. "Say, kid, yo' I saw Shorty out trying to cop some of that shit. I tried to stop her. She wouldn't listen, so instead of me shrugging my shoulders and letting her do her I decided to stay around for security just to make sure ain't nobody try and take advantage of her. You know how crooked mafuckas is in Baltimore. I knew that was yo' old lady and I just didn't wanna see her hurt. I also didn't know if you condoned the whole heroin usage. I mean she is using your product, so I was just curious."

Macho pressed the gun harder to his forehead. "George, you are my mafuckin' brother and I care about you, Dunn. But on my mother, if I ever find out you're lying to me I'm knocking yo' pasta all over the pavement, word to Cutthroat. Matter of fact." He turned his face so he could holler down the hallway. "Yo', Lashawn! Come here for a second, cutie!" He waited for her response. "Lashawn!" He frowned after waiting for ten seconds. Macho settled his eyes back on George. "Get yo sucka ass out of here. Now nigga!" He muffed him and watched George nearly break his neck to get out of the house.

As soon as he left Macho hurried to the back room and found it empty along with the rest of the house. Lashawn was long gone. He lowered his head and cursed. "What the fuck have I caused?"

Ghost

Chapter 9

"This lil' area right here is what we call Clover Land. This where my people originally come from. If a hustler getting money in Houston, he gotta know somebody that rocks out of Clover Land," Kayley informed him as she pulled the Ferrari into a parking space inside an apartment complex in the heart of Clover Land. As soon as she cut the ignition, four Shooters appeared from the side of the apartment building with black masks covering half their faces, and dark shades shielding their eyes. They carried M-16s on their sides and crept to the car like trained military men.

Preston peeped them, and slowly placed two Desert Eagles on his lap. He popped them off safety. He counted the Shooters and felt confident that he could take all four out before they were able to even get a shot off. His sole worry came in the fear of not knowing how many more were left where they came from?

"Yo, you see these niggaz creeping to the car?"

Kayley snuck her 9mm out of her purse and cocked it. "Yeah, I do. This how shit is down here, though. They just gon' make sure that we got a reason for being in the parking lot. Once we tell them that we are here to speak with Phoenix they should fall back. All these niggaz belong to the deadly Duffle Bag Cartel. You gotta watch them because they are cold-blooded as fuck just like Phoenix their leader."

"I still don't know why we meeting up with this nigga. Especially if he as shysty as you say."

"Cause he a major nigga in the real estate game, and in the dope game. We can use him to expand our portion of the Cutthroat Mafia. Macho is already doing his thing and he's making it seem like he's carrying you. I don't like no nigga thinking that he better than my man. We gon' make our own connections and turn up like that. Here they come."

All four Shooters surrounded the car. The spokesman placed the barrel of his gun to Kayley's window. "Say, Shawty roll down this window and state yo' bidness for being in Duffel Bag Cartel territory. You got a few seconds."

Kayley placed her Coronavirus mask on her face and rolled down the window. "Say, Playboy, get that bitch ass gun out my face. We here to fuck wit' Phoenix. He gave us permission to have a sit down to talk bidness. Keyword: Money up."

The Shooter mugged her for a second and then nodded his head. "Shawty, start this car up and pull it to that space right up front over there. Leave ya guns in the car. You will be pat searched and scanned with a wand. Also, no phones either, that's Phoenix's orders." He pointed at the designated space and walked backward from the car with his gun pointed at it.

"Extra ass niggaz. Always gotta make a mafucka jump through hoops just to do bidness wit' they ass," Kayley said out loud.

"Yo', you telling me that we about to still go up here and fuck wit' this nigga when we ain't gon' have no means of protection? Really, fuck type of operations he running?"

"Dis the South baby, we do shit different down here. Don't nobody trust nobody."

"I'm from out East and I don't trust a soul either. So, seeing as that's the case why am I fuckin' wit' this nigga on his terms?"

Kayley pulled into the parking spot and cut the engine. She looked over at him. "Put simply, because you ain't nothing big, right now. You making peanuts. You ain't got no clout and no real money. Don't no female wanna sit beside a bum ass nigga so it's my job to get you plugged in like a light switch so I can sit next to a boss when you finally become one. Any more questions?"

Preston was taken aback by her response. "Nall, let's go." He tucked his guns, and his phone, and she did the same.

***

Phoenix was six feet even, with caramel skin and hazel eyes. He had a low cut and deep waves that had a hint of gray in them. He was the infamous leader of the Duffel Bag Cartel, a crew of money-hungry savages that took over the dope game by gun violence, extortion, murder, and extreme bloodshed. Phoenix was personally responsible for putting more bodies underground than a gravedigger that worked countless hours of overtime. He was cold, calculating, and all about his money and didn't give a fuck about anybody that opposed him.

When they stepped into the apartment, Phoenix was already seated at the head of a long table that took up the entire living room. He puffed on a stuffed blunt of Syracuse Mango weed and mugged Kayley and Preston as they came through the door. He had two Shooters behind him that held assault rifles. Each Shooter adorned a white ski mask.

"Come on it you two and have a seat."

Preston pulled out Kayley's chair and stepped to the side sitting beside her. He nodded his head at Phoenix. "What's good?"

Phoenix ignored him for a moment. He blew smoke out of his nose. "Say, shawty, only reason I'm having this sit down is because my uncle told me to. He just touched back on the scene and he chose to lay low for the moment, but he does send his regards to you and Jackie, Kayley."

"You tell Taurus that I love him and that both me and my mother appreciate him. We're glad those people weren't able to do what they wanted to do to him." Kayley shook her head.

"Will do." Phoenix blew his smoke toward the ceiling. "So, let's get to it. The Duffel Bag Cartel is thinking 'bout growth and expansion. We hear good things 'bout Baltimore, especially when it comes to the money and the Rebirth. As you know I am the dope distributor of the Rebirth. The flow of topnotch heroin begins and ends with me."

Preston sat up in his chair. "Yo', we already got a plug on the Rebirth. We fuck wit—"

"Makaroni and Montana out of Milwaukee." Phoenix cut him off. "Yeah, those are my children, and they cop their product from me at a marked-down price. The shipment comes from Houston to Milwaukee, and then out there to you dudes in Baltimore. My question to you is, why would you want your product to take so many trips when I am the source?"

Preston frowned. "Shit this is news to me."

Phoenix laughed. "Besides, they don't fuck with you. They fuck with Macho. Your name never even came up. When I referenced you, you were described as a worker. A low level one at that."

Kayley eyed Preston. "That's why we're here. Fuck being workers. We wanna be a king and a queen. You know just like you and Natalia." Natalia was Phoenix's right-hand woman, Taurus's daughter, and the mother of his child.

Phoenix rubbed his hands together. "I see you've been doing your research. Say, Mane, I like that fire in yo' belly too, Shawty. Let's say you cross over from the Cutthroat Mafia and you come and plant yourself with the Duffel Bag Cartel. I can promise you seven figures in eighteen months."

"I'm gang gang, Cutthroat Mafia all day. Preston is my king, and my loyalty is in blood. Suwoo." Kayley let it be known.

Preston felt his heart beating fast. "A mafucka gotta be ready to die for their comments when they come at my jewel, kid. I'll murder a whole nation for my Shorty word to Jehovah."

Phoenix leaned forward and placed his hands on the table. "Yeah, that's how you feel Mane?"

"You muthafuckin' right. Loyalty and love in blood, gang gang." Preston's chest was heaving up and down.

Phoenix mugged both of them. "Say, Potna, you fuckin' wit Shawty more than you fuckin' wit' yo' homeboy back home? Macho, I think his name is?"

"That's my nigga, this my bitch. I'll kill for him, and I'll die for her. That's what that is, Kid." Preston was getting more and more riled up.

Phoenix nodded his head and eyed Preston real closely. "That sounds real sweet, but one thang 'bout the game homeboy, ain't no such thang as two heads of a mob. It's either you are the man, or you're not. It's either you gon' choose yo' bitch over yo' nigga, or vice versa. You can't do both. Shawty gon' have dilemmas that cause you to side with her more often than not, and yo' mans ain't gon' like that. When a female has a dominant opinion or presence in the decision making of a man in power it causes all other men under him to want to rebel, especially if there is a mafucka sitting beside you like Macho. Y'all ain't gon' be able to coexist once the money gets serious, and I think he knows dat. Probably why he been making major moves without your presence. Venturing out to Philly, looking at D.C. You knew 'bout all dis?" Phoenix eyed him.

Preston shook his head unmoved. "I don't give a fuck what he's doing or where he's visiting as long as the result is that it makes the Cutthroat Mafia stronger, and more financially secure. I might not have as many moons under my belt in the game as you, but I recognize a divide and conquer play when I see one. Ain't shit moving. This is Cutthroat through and through. You gon' fuck wit' us or not?"

Phoenix sat back. "You got a nice head on your shoulders. I'm surprised you caught my tactics and actually had enough gall to call me out on it. I gotta honor you for that." He laughed and then stubbed out his blunt. "Nall, but on some real shit though, you need to establish yourself as a subsection of the Cutthroat Mafia. Your mans handling his bidness already. On the strength of your lady, her mother, and my uncle, Taurus, I would like to extend my hand in partnership.

"With the Duffel Bag Cartel behind you, you'll be able to get birds of the Rebirth for the low. Troops that come out there on the sole mission to conquer and annihilate for you, and our protection. I can help you navigate through the game until you become a Titan amongst Lords. But Mane, I'm telling you when you see, Jackie you gotta thank her for what she did for my uncle Taurus. Everythang starts wit' her." He scooted away from the table and walked until he was standing in front of Preston with his hand out.

Preston stood up and shook his hand. "It's an honor, Phoenix. Before I leave this building, I would like for us to get a full understanding of each other and how business will look from here on out. You cool wit' that."

Phoenix shook his hand and released it. "I wouldn't accept it any other way, let's begin."

Chapter 10

Four hours later, Preston pulled his shirt over his head and dropped his bulletproof vest to the floor. He stepped out of his clothes until he was naked and slipped into the shower behind Kayley who was already inside it allowing the water to bead into her face. He sucked on the back of her neck and cupped her naked breasts.

"Damn, I missed these, the nipples are so long." He pulled on them, rubbed her breasts in a circular motion, and kissed her neck.

"Mmm, I knew we wasn't gon' be able to just shower without you putting your hands on me." She smiled and wiggled her booty against his front.

Preston grew hard, he rubbed it up and down the crease of her booty. "Baby, tell me what Jackie did for that nigga, Taurus that Phoenix was talking about? Who is Taurus anyway?" He slipped his hands down and played with the lips of her pussy, opening them and allowing the water to drum on her erect clitoris.

"My mother helped him escape and fake his death." She turned around to face him. "You sure you wanna talk about that instead of getting some of this pinkness? We ain't fucked in almost two weeks."

Preston gripped her ass and brought her front to the tip of his piece. "Yo', I definitely wanna know how this story goes, but we can wait. I ain't bugging." He pushed her against the wall roughly and dropped down. She placed her right foot on the rim of the tub. Preston rubbed her pussy and stuck his nose on the lips and sniffed hard. "Damn, I love the natural smell of yo' cat."

Kayley giggled. "You better." She looked down at him. "Why you drop down? So, you could get a better view or somethin'?"

"Better view my ass, I wanna taste this box." He opened her lips wide and sucked on it.

His tongue slid into her pink, she moaned and he darted it in and out at full speed. His nose bumped into her clitoris. He licked circles around it, before sucking it into his lips.

Kayley grabbed his head and began to hump into his face. "Make me cum, daddy. Make me cum. Unnnn! Unnnn! Make me cum, fuck!" Her nipples poked out a full inch while water dripped off the tips of them.

Preston held her sex lips apart and gave her the best head of her life for thirty minutes straight. She moaned and she screamed as she came all over his neck. She stopped to tongue him down just so she could taste herself.

Preston stood up and placed his dick head on to her lips. "Here, baby girl. Do daddy."

Kayley sat on the edge of the tub bobbing her head back and forth into his lap. She slurped louder and louder while his toes curled. She popped his dick out stroking it with her left hand. "You like that, daddy, huh? You like how yo' baby gets down?" She slurped him back into her mouth.

Preston was whimpering with his hand holding the shower walls. He shivered and was ready to blow. The sight of Kayley's perfect B cup titties was driving him crazy. The more she sucked it, it appeared that her nipples got longer and longer. Preston grabbed a handful of her hair and was about to blow when Jackie knocked on the door and came into the bathroom at the same time. She stood staring in disbelief at her little girl.

"Oh, shit, I'm sorry, baby. I gotta pee."

Kayley popped Preston out of her mouth and kept stroking his dick. "Gon' head, mama. This yo' house, ain't nobody stopping you, long as you know I'm grown and you ain't finna stop me either."

Jackie shook her head and lifted the toilet seat. She pulled her night-gown up around her waist facing them and started to do her business. "Y'all just act like I ain't even here."

Kayley licked up and down, Preston's dick. She moaned deep in her throat. "What do you say, Preston? You scared 'bout my mama being in the room while I do this?" She sucked him back into her mouth deep throating him at full speed now. She closed her eyes and went to work.

Jackie moaned and slid her hand between her thighs. She fingered her clitoris. She jerked on the toilet and scooted forward with her eyes on the size of Preston's dick. "He's so handsome, baby." She spaced her thighs further apart.

Preston humped into Kayley's mouth at full speed. "Uh! Uh! Uh!" He began to shake looking directly at Jackie's fat pussy.

Kayley popped him out and stood up. She stepped out of the tub and bent over the sink. "'Bout to introduce you to how we get down in the south, daddy. Get yo' ass back here and fuck me in front of my mama. All she's been talking 'bout is the length of yo' dick ever since she's seen you in yo' boxers. Ain't it, mama?"

Jackie sucked her dripping fingers after pulling them out of herself. "He's such a fine young man. Damn, they don't make 'em like dat no mo."

Kayley smacked herself on the ass. "Come on, Preston, fuck me in front of my mama."

Preston climbed out of the tub and got behind her. Before he could line himself up, Jackie took a hold of his dick and sucked it into his mouth. She slid all the way to the bottom of it and brought it back out then sucked it down again fondling his sack.

She moaned. "Okay, son. Now fuck my baby."

Her spit dripped off his dick along with precum. Preston shivered as he lined himself up in disbelief of what Jackie had done. He pushed the head into Kayley slowly and yanked her back to him implanting her pussy on his dick. She screamed. He dug his fingers into her waist and proceeded to fuck her like an animal, long stroking.

Tack! Tack! Tack! Tack!

Their skins slapped together over and over. Kayley's pussy queefed and leaked down his stalk. Her fat ass jiggled with each plunge. She arched her back and pushed back faster and faster. Preston spaced his feet and fucked her harder and faster growling like an angry lion.

Jackie stood up with her fingers deep inside of her. She walked beside Preston and rubbed his back. She licked the shower water and the mounting sweat from his flesh. Then she sucked on his neck and rubbed the sides of his dick every time it slid into Kayley. She collected their juices off his balls and sucked her fingers clean, moaning around them.

Kayley looked back and saw Jackie and Preston making out, she growled, then came. Jackie's big booty was in her face. She could see her juicy pussy lips leaking their essence and the sight brought on another rolling orgasm.

She shivered. "Unnnn! Unnnn! Mama! He's killing me. He's killing yo' baby. Look at his dick! Look at it going in and out of meeee!" She came again.

Preston fucked and fucked, he felt Jackie licking his booty and it caused him to squirm. She bit the back of his left thigh. He came jerking uncontrollably. His knees got weak and he fell against Kayley's back.

"Aw, fuck! Fuck!" He pulled his dick out ready to buss on her back some.

Jackie took a hold of it and sucked it into her mouth. She tasted his seed and it spurred her on to suck harder and faster. She pumped and squeezed her fist. Every time a drop of his seed dripped, she savored it on her tongue until there was no more. She groaned in disappointment. She sucked him for two full minutes afterward and popped him out of her mouth with him standing tall and firm. She rubbed the head on her pussy lips pushing it slightly into herself and pulling it back out greasy from her juices.

Kayley watched her. "Don't do it, mama. He gon' be my husband. I can't let you fuck my husband. That wouldn't be right."

Jackie spread her thick thighs and slipped Preston's dick head into her hotness two slight inches. "Please, baby girl. I won't say anything. Besides, every man wanna know what his mother-in-law pussy feels like, ask him." She kissed Preston's lips.

He grabbed her ass and humped his hips forward sliding four inches into her hot, wet pussy. His eyelids fluttered.

"Awww, please, baby daughter. Please, I'll do anything," Jackie begged.

Kayley rubbed her own slit. Her juices and Preston's cum slid down her inner thighs. "Mama, you can't. Now let him go so we can get some sleep. He gon' be my husband. We can't do it like that." She grabbed Preston and pulled his dick out of her.

Preston whimpered and groaned, pissed off. His piece jumped up and down hungrily. "Damn, yo', if ain't shit happening then I needed to get up out of this bathroom. Yo moms mad fine and her gap is fire. Word to God." He took one last glance at Jackie's pussy before he left out of the bathroom.

Jackie walked up to Kayley and swiped her slit with her fingers. She sucked the digits into her mouth. "I thought we were family and we shared everythang? Guess there are certain exceptions to the rule all of a sudden. Wasn't like that wit' Taurus, though, hmmph!" She bumped her and pulled her gown down before she left the bathroom.

Kayley stood with her head lowered shaking it for five minutes before she joined Preston in the bedroom. She found him beating his meat with his eyes closed. "Hey, boy! What the fuck are you doing?"

Preston stopped and laid on his back. He was breathing hard. "Yo', I ain't never seen shit so hot in my life. This that shit that you only read about in all of those books by Ghost. I never thought it really happened for real. Now that I see it do I gotta cum while the moment is still hot in my mind." He went back to beating himself.

Kayley crawled across the bed. "Wait, let me sit on it while her juices still all over the tip." She straddled him and sank down in one motion. "Unnnhhh shit!" She placed her hands on his chest. "You wanted to fuck my mama, didn't you?"

Preston rubbed her ass. "Just cause she yo' mama. That shit hot. Now come on, ride me."

Kayley moaned and jumped forward. "Uh! Uh! What if? What if I let you?" She rode him faster.

She reached out and took a hold of the headboard rolling her back, imagining Preston pounding Jackie out. She moaned and bit into her bottom lip.

Preston grabbed her ass and forced her to ride him faster and faster. He tried not to pay attention to the things that were coming out of her mouth because they would cause him to cum prematurely. Kayley's pussy was good, and the fact that both her and Jackie's naked bodies were fresh in his mind he wanted to enjoy their romp for as long as he could. "Uh fuck!"

"You. You. You, heard me?" Kayley threw her head back and moaned with her mouth wide open. She rolled her back faster and faster.

Preston bounced her up and down. "If. If. You gon' let me then let me." He rolled her over and forced her knees to her chest. He started to fuck her with all his might slamming into her middle. She was so wet that her juices were popping up and splashing before it ran down and drenched the bed. Preston dug as deep as he could for three minutes and came again. He jerked over and over, then fell on top of her with his hips rising and falling.

Kayley's thick thighs were wide open. She shivered and laid there. "Damn, you so nasty. I'ma think about it. I do wanna throw her bone, and who better than her son-in-law." She sat up and tongued him down while he slowly stroked her to another earth-shattering orgasm.

Ghost

Chapter 11

The next morning Preston woke up to find Kayley already awake. She was laying beside him rubbing his stomach. The room was still dark because the blinds were closed, but specks of the sunlight were visible.

"Preston, you 'member you were asking me how it was that my mama helped Taurus get out of his jam?"

Preston yawned and stretched his arms. His head was pounding. The Percocets were calling out to him. "Yeah, what about it, Shorty?"

Kayley kissed his stomach. "Well, the first thing you need to know is everything I'm about to tell you stays between us. A'ight, that's the first thing and it is very important. Can you honor that?"

Preston looked down at her. "Yeah, I got you. Hold on, let me pop a few Perks first."

Kayley handed him two sixties. "I already knew you were gon' get to it right away so here and listen to me." She handed him a glass of water.

Preston crushed the pills with his teeth and made a sour face when he swallowed them. The crushing of them would help him feel the effects sooner than later. He was still trying to avoid tooting them like so many of his comrades in Baltimore including, Macho.

"Yo, do ya thing Shorty, I'm all ears like a field of corn."

Kayley rolled her eyes. "Whatever." Then she got the metaphor and laughed. "That was clever. Anyway."

"Start by telling me who Taurus is."

"Okay." She took a deep breath. "Taurus is a drug lord and a legend out of Memphis, Tennessee. He started out as a young kid, cursed with an abusive father, an abused mother, a poor family, and all kinds of odds stacked against him. He found a way to take those odds and shoot to the top of the game."

Preston shrugged his shoulders. "And? So, what. That nigga sound like every other hustler that done made a few million in the game after coming from nothing. What so good about him?" Preston wasn't impressed so far.

"Well, Taurus was different. When he jumped off the porch to get money, he didn't do it for himself. He did it for his mother first, then his little sister Marie. She was killed by the way. Another thing about Taurus was that as soon as he jumped into the game the men in his family began to hunt to kill him in every way that they could. They were jealous, spiteful, evil, and unfair to both him and his mother.

"Their actions would cause Taurus to over plot and find a plethora of ways to crush and murder them until he had completely decimated them. Legend has it that he killed both of his brothers and woulda killed his father if his mother hadn't got to him first. You see, his father was a cruel man that had a habit of beating his children and his wife into the ground. Before Taurus entered the game his father was already in it, but the other hustlers never really honored nor respected him like they did, Taurus. I think that crushed his ego."

"Okay—so why do niggaz honor blood so much? I still don't get it."

"Because it was Taurus that paved a way for all of the real money getting cliques out of Memphis. The Duffel Bag Cartel that runs under Phoenix. The Bread Gang that Moneybagg the rapper claims, the Rotten to the Core crew outta Philly, and the Drug Lords out of Milwaukee that runs under Makaroni. These are just to name a few. When he plugged The Rebirth into the slums of Memphis especially White Haven, and Orange Mound he helped a bunch of dudes get on and get money.

He was the root, and I've found out that he is still just as strong as he was before he was indicted for double murder."

"*Double murder.* Damn, how blood come from under that jam?"

"He didn't, he faked his death and escaped, before reemerging." She took a deep breath. "Preston, Taurus is my father. He is the sole reason why the Duffel Bag Cartel had been given the go ahead to plug you into the game. He wants to meet you when the time is right, but that's after you prove yourself worthy to do so."

Preston slipped out of the bed. "*Prove myself?* Fuck is you talking about? I ain't gotta prove myself to no nigga." He was vexed.

Kayley tried to keep her cool. "First of all, he isn't a nigga, he's my father, and I love him. I'm just starting to get into his life and he just wants the best for me and my future. You see this shit is no different if we were all legit. This is the game, and in this game we Stevens are royalty, but we don't believe in handouts. We get money on our own branches and we get a lot of it. I am a female, yet a Queen. You are going to be my kings that's why I gotta make sure you now represent our family well."

"So, dis shit all about you then? Go figure. Yo, word to God, I don't need no bitch turning over stones for me. I can get it on my own. Now I can respect that ya pops is a major nigga and all of that, but on my blood, I can get it on my own." He slipped into his boxers.

"Fuck that. You ain't gotta. Damn, are you so fuckin' pig-headed that you can't take a blessing when it's punching yo' goofy ass right in the face?" She scoffed and stepped into his face. "You fuckin' wit' a bitch that got royal blood. I'm deeply rooted in the game through my pops, and you will be, too. I ain't just thinking 'bout no sorry ass Baltimore or even Philly.

I'm thinking 'bout taking over the game state by state along with the real estate market. We can make some legal investments, and really run up a check before we cash out. My sister can sing like an Angel, my pops already getting her signed with Bread Gang. If Megan Thee Stallion's ugly ass can make a profit, why wouldn't Kim-Kim be able to?"

Preston laughed. "That bitch is popped, though. Yo, I swear she looks strong as hell. All that shit fake, too. You can tell." He laughed.

"See what I'm saying, and my father Taurus is the whole reason that bitch doing stupid numbers in the game. He pushing Moneybagg and Gotti. That's that behind the scenes money getting to the fullest." She rubbed his chest. "Baby, I ain't trying to run you, but I do wanna see us thrive. Can you please fall in line for a minute? Just go hard in the game with my guidance that is going to come straight from him, and we'll prosper. Can you tuck your tail? Please for me?" Her brown eyes searched his with her bottom lip poked out.

Preston kissed it and pulled her closer to him by her ass. He tongued her down. "Yo, I'll do anything for you. You want the God to follow behind ya old man, as long as it is highly beneficial then I'm wit' it, word up."

Kayley squealed and wrapped her arms around his neck. She kissed his lips over and over again. "Thank you, thank you, thank you." She stepped back and held his hands. "Since you chose to do the right thing I guess I can introduce you to how my bloodline gets down. There is another part of the story that I left out, but I'll let my mother explain it to you. She's waiting for you in her room. Good luck."

Preston's eyes got as big as saucers. "Yo', stop, you finna let me wax moms?"

Kayley sat on the bed and opened her thighs. "Unless you wanna stay here and fuck me instead?"

Preston leaned down and kissed her forehead. "No take-backs." He ran out of the room. "Jackie! Jackie! Where you at, shorty? I got permission."

Kayley sat on the bed feeling more rejected than a girl not asked to the prom. "Well, fuck you den, Preston. Don't ask me for no ass later." She got up and slammed the door.

Preston didn't hear the last part; he was too busy turning the doorknob of Jackie's room. He stuck his head in and smelled the perfume that met him. Her room was dimly lit. "Yo', Ms. Jackie?"

Jackie was sitting in the middle of the bed with her thick thighs wide open. Her pussy was freshly shaved and puffy. She had a glass of white wine in her left hand and a joint in her right. "Come on in, son."

Preston stepped into the room and closed the door. He walked beside the bed. "On some real shit, I've been wanting to get between these thighs since I first laid eyes on you. You super thick. Can I taste that pussy?"

She opened her thighs wider. "Lusting over your girl's mother is indecent. What type of man are you?"

"A real one." Preston crawled on the bed and pulled her closer to him.

He stuck his head between her thighs and kissed her naked pussy lips smashing them inward. He licked up and down the folds until he spread her wide open and paid specific attention to her clit. She arched her back and put down both the wine and the joint. Preston kept munching.

"Uh-huh. Uh-huh, ooo, you gon' love this family baby. I'ma make sure of that." She forced his face further into her gap, while she watched him do his thing.

Preston turned his head sideways and slid two fingers in and out of her, digging deeper and deeper each time. "I can't wait to fuck this pussy. I ain't never met an older woman this thick before. You sexy as fuck." He slurped her gap for ten minutes straight and stuck his tongue into her as far as it could go while his nose bumped against her clitoris purposely.

Jackie laid on her back and rode his face moaning louder and louder. She wrapped her ankles around the back of his neck and trapped him. "Unnnn! Unnnn! Baby! Babeeeee! I'm cumming! I'm cumming!" She locked him in place and screamed.

Preston couldn't breathe but he kept right on licking and sucking. He couldn't believe Kayley had given him the green light. His piece was so hard that it hurt. When she finally released his face, he inhaled a breath of fresh air and jumped on top of her. "N'all, don't run, bring that ass here." He fell between her thighs and fingered her at full speed. She moaned louder. Her juices were overflowing like never before. Preston removed his fingers and got in place after stripping. He placed his dick on her entrance and slammed it home.

"Uhhhhh, fuck, lil' baby!" Jackie hollered arching her back. She grabbed him around the neck and pulled him down so she could kiss all over his lips. They kissed loudly while Preston stroked faster and faster digging as deep as he could. "Harder, baby." More kissing. Her tongue swiped across his lips, then she licked all over his neck, before biting into it. "Uh-huh! Uhhh! Uhhh! Fuck me harder, baby!"

Preston pressed her knees to her shoulders and watched his piece go in and out of her at full speed. She was leaking. Her juices caused a clear string of precum to stick to his piece. It plunged in and out opening her sex lips wide. He leaned down.

"I was just fuckin' your daughter like this," he growled. *Bam! Bam! Bam! Bam!* "I was just fuckin' yo baby."

"Uhhhh, shut up! Shut up. Uhhh, Kayley come get this boy. Please! Unnnnnn, he fuckin' the shit out of me." Her ankles beat on the back of his shoulders.

Preston dug deeper, he fell between her thighs stroking. He flipped her on her side and kept fucking. Pressing her right thigh to her rib cage. "You a thick ass bitch, mama." *Bam! Bam! Bam!* "Awww you so fuckin' thick!" He curled his back, and grabbed a hold of her for grip, banging into her as hard as he could. Her pussy gripped him and worked toward milking him.

Jackie had tears coming out of her eyes from the sheer pleasure of the act. She rubbed his chest and helped to hold her thigh up for him. He was banging so deep, scratching surfaces that hadn't been scratched in a long time. She twisted out of his hold and pushed him to the bed, straddled him, and slid his pipe back into herself.

"You want this pussy? Mama gon' give it to you just like this." She rode him biting his chest. Her ass popped, her thighs tightened around his sides, and she kept on bucking feeling him pushing at her lower belly. She slammed down harder and faster. "Uhhh! Uhhhh! It's so good. It's so good, uh, you my son in law." She sat up and screamed at the top of her lungs, cumming in violent tremors. Tears ran down her cheeks. She felt Preston bussing inside her before she fell on his chest breathing hard.

Preston rolled her off him and straddled her body. He looked down at her. "Damn you so mafuckin' gorgeous. At least I know what Kayley gon' look like when she gets in her forties." He kissed her lips.

She smiled. "Well, thank you, baby." She pulled him down and laid beside him rubbing his chest. "Preston, I know this whole arrangement might seem a bit weird to you, but this is just what it is. We are southern girls, and our family is close-knit. Kayley in particular comes from a bloodline that does things their own way. Sometimes she may have urges inside her that even she doesn't understand. It's for you to support her through it, and for you to know that she loves you with all her heart. She has never told me that she's felt this way about a man until you."

Kayley stepped in the doorway. "Yeah, Preston. So, you better get your mind right." She walked over to the bed and laid in between them. "You feel better, mama?" She stroked her cheek.

Jackie nodded. "Yeah, I do. Thank you, baby. Now y'all gon' and get up out of here before I get to asking for round two. That boy is somethin' else." She kissed Kayley's lips and then tongued Preston down for two straight minutes.

Chapter 12

It was a bright and sunny afternoon, on a hot and humid Wednesday. Macho was rolling his Benz truck through the streets of Baltimore on his way to checking on a few traps when he rolled down Colgate Avenue and saw Lashawn staggering out of the alley. She tried her best to fix the dirty windbreaker that was halfway on her shoulder. She cursed at the difficulty of it. When she made it on to the block, she stopped for a second holding her stomach. She hurried to the grass, fell to her knees, and pushed her guts loudly. She threw up very little and ended with a series of dry heaves. She'd lost fifteen pounds, and her hair was thinner, and in a mess.

Macho felt his heart drop into his stomach. "Yo', I know that ain't Lashawn, B?" He rolled away from the stop sign and drove toward her. The closer he got the sicker he became until he was jumping out of the truck and running around it. He stopped standing over her. "Yo', Lashawn, what the fuck happened to you, goddess?"

Lashawn looked up at him and ran her fingers through her unkempt hair. "Macho." She stood up and shielded her eyes from the sun. The sour aroma coming from her body was proof that she hadn't showered in a full two weeks.

Macho looked her up and down, his eyes became misty. "Baby, what's the matter? How can I help you?"

Lashawn glared at him. "Aw, so now all of a sudden you wanna help me, huh?" She stood in his face. "Don't nobody give a fuck about me or my baby. All y'all care about are yourselves!" She hollered sticking her finger in his face.

Macho knocked it away. "Yo', that's a lie and you know it. I tried to snatch ya ass up weeks ago, but you wound up running out the backdoor. But I ain't letting you get away this time. You coming wit' me. I wanna help you." He took a hold of her arm.

Lashawn snatched her arm away from him and pushed him as hard as she could. "I don't need yo' fuckin' pity you son of a bitch! Not yours, not Preston's, not nobody's. I got this." She turned around to walk away from him, grew woozy, and staggered into the light pole holding herself up.

Macho lowered his head for a moment. His temper began to flare. He had every intention of walking away from her and leaving her to fend for herself. Then he thought about the fact that the reason she was going off on the deep end was because of what happened to Lashonda. He was sure of that, and if that was the case he knew without a shadow of a doubt that it was his fault. He allowed her to get halfway down the block before he took off running behind her.

When he caught up to her, he stepped into her face. "Yo', Lashawn, I been fucking up. I know I shoulda been there for you more than what I have been. I left you to fend for yourself and it's been wrong of me. You deserve better, and I promise that from here on out that's what I am going to render to you. Come here." He pulled her into his embrace. The scent of her was so strong that he could barely breathe, but he fought through his wooziness.

Lashawn allowed him to hold her for a moment, then suddenly she wiggled up out of his embrace and pushed him away. "I don't wanna be saved, Macho. I'm fucked up right now. I ain't got no baby girl no more, no money, and no purpose for breathing." She shook her head and laughed. "I sat around talking about how I was independent and I stood on my own two feet when in actuality I ain't never had nothing. I ain't never been nothing, and I ain't never gon' amount to nothing because those were the cards that I was dealt. I was born to lose, just like my mama." She wiped her dry lips that were lightly bleeding. "I appreciate you taking time out of your day to try and rescue me, but this is one damsel that can't be rescued. I wanna die, and that's what I'm working on." She pulled up the sleeve of her jacket to show him her arm. There were track marks everywhere. She looked up at him to see his reaction.

Macho was in tears. "Yo', I should kick your mafuckin' ass. You ain't acting like nothing but a punk." He snatched her up by her shirt and pulled a .45 out of his holster. He pressed the barrel to her forehead with tears running down his cheeks. "You wanna give up, huh?"

Lashawn nodded. "Kill me. Please kill me. Send me up there with my daughter. I don't wanna be here no more."

Macho clenched his teeth. "Yo', I should waste you, Lashawn. I should blow this coward ass head right off your shoulders."

Lashawn leaned her face forward. "Fuck is you waiting on then? Do it. Do it. I don't wanna be here no more, Macho. They killed my daughter. What kind of a mother can't even protect her own child?" She covered her face with her hands. "He wasn't even supposed to have had her. I let her go with him on a day that wasn't even his and she's dead because of me." She slumped to the ground crying her eyes out. The water from her tears left dirt streaks all over her face.

Macho tucked his gun and saw that there were numerous people peeking out of their windows on the block. There was one old man sitting on his porch rocking in his chair and smoking a tobacco pipe watching the whole scene as if it was nothing more than a ghetto soap opera. Macho picked, a crying Lashawn up, and carried her to his truck. He pulled the seat belt around her and closed the door. He ran around and got in the truck and pulled off.

That night he stripped her naked and helped her ease into his tub that he'd already added bath salts too. He took a loofah and scrubbed the dirt from her body. He allowed the dirty water to drain out of the tub before he helped her stand up. He turned on the shower and washed her from head to toe. When he was done, he carried her from the shower to the bedroom where he laid her down and lotioned her body. After finishing that, he fed her a light meal of chicken noodle soup. She drank apple juice before they hugged up in the bed. Lashawn snuggled into his chest. She was emotional, slightly disoriented, yet she felt safe and secure within him. Macho kissed her forehead.

"Macho?" Lashawn began to shake.

Macho rubbed her side and pressed his lips on the side of her forehead. "What's good, baby?"

"Baby, thank you for doing all of this for me, but I gotta be honest. That heroin is calling me, I'm shaking. My stomach is in knots. I can't help but think about how it will feel flowing through my veins. I need it, I gotta have it. I'll be back, I just gotta go get right." She came from under his embrace and scooted toward the edge of the bed.

Macho dropped his head. "N'all, shorty, you ain't going nowhere. I'ma chill here with you, and we gon' break that habit cold turkey."

Lashawn stood up and looked at him with a bit of fear. "Macho, I know you care about me, but you can't possibly understand what I'm going through, right now. My insides feel like they're being twisted like silly putty." She began to get dressed. "Now I'm all for kicking this habit in time, but I ain't finna do shit cold turkey, that's just nuts." She put on her shoes and opened the bedroom door.

Two big, beefy killers that were employed by the Cutthroat Mafia stood on guard. One of them grabbed the door handle from her and slammed the door back. She stepped back, caught off guard.

Macho laid on the bed with his hands behind his head. "I love you way too fuckin' much to see you allow this drug to get the better of you. Word to God, you ain't leaving this mafucka until that shit is out of your system. Now get ya ass back in the bed."

Lashawn felt like crying. She rushed to the bedroom window and pulled the curtains back. The window was covered with bars. She growled and balled her fists. "Macho, please!"

Macho stood up. "Yo', when a man loves a woman, he'll do anything for her. I told you that if you ever crossed over to me that I would hold you down against all odds. That shit is still in full effect. Now bring ya ass over here and get in the bed."

Lashawn pulled the window all the way up and shook the bars. She punched the fiberglass to no avail. She turned away from the window and tried to pull the door back open. One of the big guards kept a hold on it. She screamed and fell to her knees. Her stomach spasmed. She heaved and tasted the chicken noodle soup that she'd consumed earlier.

"Kill me, Macho. Get yo' black ass up and kill me right now, please." She rocked back and forth on her calve muscles.

Macho got out of the bed and dropped down to his knees. "Baby, right now you are low. As your man, this is where I wanna meet you, right in the eye of your storm. You may be here right now but together we are going to get back up there. I'ma pick you up like I'm supposed to."

"No! You don't understand, Macho." She jumped up and rushed him swinging wildly. Her punches caught him all over the face and neck. She swung and swung until she got sick. She rushed to the bathroom and threw up in the toilet over and over. Then she fell to the floor and curled into a ball. "Why are you doing me like this, Macho? You said you loved me. You said that you would never hurt me. Well, this hurts. My insides are killing me, and you don't even care." She began to sweat profusely.

Macho wiped the blood from his nose. He took off his black beater and walked into the bathroom with his muscles popping, and tattoos all over his body. He squatted down on the floor and got behind her. He pulled her back to him and wrapped his arms around her body. "I love you, Goddess. I ain't 'bout to let you be defeated. I ain't 'bout to allow no weapon formed against you to prosper. Word to Jehovah, Goddess." He kissed the back of her neck.

Lashawn shivered even harder now. "I don't want your help. I don't want anybody's help. I just wanna get high. I wanna take the pain away. I'm tired of this feeling. Why can't you just leave me alone?" she cried.

Macho kissed her. "When a man loves a woman, he'll kill for her. He'll die for her. He will rescue her with everything that he is. I left you, I led you down this path because I left you for a minute. So, it's my job to rescue you. I ain't going nowhere. Word up."

Lashawn was in tears now. She threw up and didn't even make it to the toilet. Her body was suffering from cold sweats, then she would get hot, then cold again. She tried to get up, but Macho kept her bound. "Please, Macho. You don't need to love me. I don't even love you. Get the fuck off me. Just let me go."

"Yo', I'ma love you until you are strong enough to love yourself. I need you Lashawn, I crave you. You are my whole world. I ain't about to let you be crushed by this demon. Fuck that."

Lashawn threw her head back to try and buss his face. She tried to mule kick him in the nuts, but he blocked her attacks. He shielded himself from the harm and kept a hold of her.

"Ahhhhhh, I hate you." She trembled sweating. She imagined the syringe going into her arm, and dry heaved ten times in a row.

She scratched at her arms, then she tried to suck remnants of the Heroin from her injection sites even though she knew it was impossible. She needed to get Macho off her. She needed to make him hate her. She wracked her brain for something that would piss him off. She felt dizzy and nauseous. Then it clicked.

She swallowed her cotton mouth spit. "I fucked George."

Macho was holding her tight, and slightly released her. "Fuck you say?"

"I said I fucked George without a condom. I might be pregnant by him." She felt Macho release her entirely before he stood up. She smiled, wiped her mouth, and sat up. "I want his baby. I'm in love with him," she lied.

Macho mugged her for a long time. He balled his hands into fists and exhaled, before grabbing her by the hair and picking her up slamming her against the wall. "Lashawn, you better not be playing wit' me cause you 'bout to make me do some shit that I really don't wanna do."

"I'm grown, ain't nobody playing wit' yo black ass. Now get your filthy hands off me. I wanna go be with my baby daddy." She knocked his hands away and pulled open the bathroom door. She closed it behind her and felt elated when Macho didn't step out of it. She rushed to get fully dressed. She hurried to the bedroom door and grew pissed when she found it still being held by the security guard. "Can you tell your punk ass security to get away from the door?"

Macho came out of the bathroom with a sunken expression on his face. He wanted to throw up imagining filthy ass George on top of his woman. How could she sleep with his brother? How could she stoop so low? He hated the sight of her face. "Put that shit on Lashonda that you slept with that disgusting ass nigga. Put that shit on that baby's grave and I'll let you go, you have my word."

Lashawn nodded. "On Lashonda, I screwed him. I don't know if I'm pregnant or not, but I could be because—"

Macho closed the distance between them and clamped his hand over her mouth. He picked her up and slammed her to the wall. He placed his hand around her neck and squeezed with his eyes pinned on the floor of the bedroom. He tried his best to calm down. She gagged and hit at his hands. Macho squeezed some more.

"Lashawn, I swear to God you broke my heart. I don't know why you would let that nigga between your legs but what's done is done. I love you, and I wish the best for you." He kissed her crusty lips and let her go.

She fell to her knees struggling to breathe, holding her neck. "You fuckin' psycho!"

Macho beat on the door. "Yo', let shorty out, she's dismissed. No coverage either." This meant that no one from the Cutthroat Mafia was to follow her for security purposes. He was releasing her back into the world on her own.

Lashawn got up and stepped into the hallway once the door opened. "I'm sorry, Macho. He caught me when I was vulnerable. I didn't mean to cross you like that. I was just—"

Macho slammed the door. "Have a nice life, Lashawn."

Lashawn mugged the door for a long time. She broke out into tears. She cried for three full minutes in front of it and then she grew angry. She kicked the door. "Some man you are! Fuck you, though, Macho. I knew you ain't give a fuck about me!" She stormed out of the house.

Ghost

Chapter 13

It was two days after Macho had kicked her out of his place. Lashawn sat on the floor of George's filthy living room with her back against the wall. She pushed the syringe into her vein and pushed down on the feeder that fed the heroin into her bloodstream. Her eyes rolled into the back of her head. She felt blissful. She pulled the syringe out and licked her injection site. She closed her eyes and began to nod out.

George stood over her with a big smile on his face. He kneeled and sat beside her. He pulled a fifty sack of the Re-birth from his pocket and waved it in front of her face. "Lashawn, baby, guess who has a surprise for you?" He sang in a cheerful voice.

Lashawn opened her eyes into slits. "Who baby?" She tried to focus her vision. Her speech slurred and her mouth was dry as the desert.

"Me, boo." He leaned over and licked her face. "Huh, I'ma give you this dope after I wax that big ass. Come on, let's go to the back room and do our thang." He helped her to her feet. When she got there, he wrapped his arm around her waist and allowed her to lean on him. He guided her to the backroom with his hands on her ass, squeezing and groping.

***

Macho pulled into the back alley of George's duplex. He got out of the car, grabbed his black leather gloves off the passenger's seat. He put them on and took a hold of the golf club from the back seat. He slammed the door to his car, and jogged through George's backyard, along the side of the house, and onto his front porch. He twisted the knob and smiled evilly when he found the door unlocked. He pushed it inward with anger and fury coursing through his system. He tiptoed through the house in search of the pair.

***

"Come on, bitch. Stop playin' wit' me. You ain't finna keep shooting up my shit and not give up the pussy. Now come on and don't make me take this shit. He ripped her long tee shirt off her and pinned her to the bed. Next came her panties. Lashawn began to fight him back. This only excited George. He pulled off his boxers and punched her in the nose busting it.

Lashawn was so high that she didn't feel the pain of the assault. She kicked her legs wildly with blood flowing down her cheek. "Get off me, George! Please, get off me!" she screamed.

George situated himself between her thighs and was about to slip into her when the bedroom door burst open, and Macho stepped into the room. He cocked back the golf club and swung it with so much velocity that when it connected with the back of George's head, Macho fell to one knee with blood spattered across his face. George flew on top of Lashawn and rolled to the carpet gushing.

Lashawn screamed. "Oh, my God! Oh, my God!" She scooted away from Macho.

Macho stood over George. "Bitch ass nigga! You wanna rape hoez, huh? That's what you wanna do?"

George crawled around on the floor discombobulated, then he used the bed to help him come to a standstill. The back of his head was opened like a barn door. "What did you do to me? Why the fuck you hit me bitch?"

Macho dropped the gold club. "Yo', Lashawn, I'm sorry ma'. I can't give up on you. I know this bitch ass nigga had everything to do with you falling victim to that shit." He waited until George stood up.

He cocked back and punched him as hard as he could knocking him into the wall. George made a big hole. He swung lazily over and over. Macho grabbed him and flung him to the floor. He straddled his body and drained down punches on him over and over breaking his jaw, busting his mouth and nose, and eventually knocking him out cold. He stepped over him and took hold of Lashawn.

"Come on, you coming with me. And this time I ain't letting you go."

***

Preston cast back his fishing line and whipped it forward as far as it could go. This was his first time on a Yacht and it felt relaxing to him. Growing up he'd always wanted his father to take him fishing. He'd always wanted to bond with the man but was never given the opportunity because his father was just one of those types of men that didn't care about his children or the things that they wanted. This was another reason why Preston couldn't wait until he had his first child so that he could do all of the things with it that he'd yearned for his parents to do with him when he was a boy.

Kayley strolled on to the deck, the bright sunlight reflected off her forehead and Chanel glasses. She handed Preston a glass of pink lemonade. "How you doing out here, baby? You feeling like a boss or what?"

Preston smiled and nodded his head to the Kim-Kim's track that was coming out of the speakers. "It's good, cutie. Yo, if I could, I would come out here every day and fish. This shit super relaxing."

Kayley laughed. "Yeah, well, it's unfortunate but the real bosses that get that major money in the game rarely ever get to lounge like this. This is why I'm making sure that we enjoy ourselves right now because after we get back to Baltimore it's about to be all about the grind."

Kim-Kim came out of the cabin wearing a two-piece all-white Prada G-string swimsuit. She danced to her own music and eased on to the deck in front of the pair. "Shawty dats a hit right there. I can't wait until that hits the charts." She closed her eyes and nodded her head.

Preston's eyes were pinned on the front of her panties. Her camel toe was visible. The one-piece was all up in her gap, and Kim-Kim was already strapped, southern thick. "Yo', you can thank the kid for helping you get plugged in with them Bread Gang niggaz."

Kim-Kim placed her hand on her hip. "Thank you for what? They let it be known right away that the only reason they bumped my demos to the top of the line is because they owed a favor to Taurus. Now once they heard me sang, they said that was all me. So, please explain to me how you fit into this equation?" she asked.

"I told ya sister. She grew interested because of me. Then I hollered at Phoenix, who in turn hollered at Taurus, who got them Bread Gang niggaz to play ball. Just so happens that the reason they signed you so quickly is cause they just found out that my section of the Cutthroat Mafia will be their plug from here on out. Anythang they cop goes through me. When I get back to Baltimore them niggaz gotta check in with the chapter out there. Bagg and 'nem supposed to be moving to Atlanta to fuck wit' Baby. That nigga Baby gotta follow suit too. Our mafia about to put the vice grips on all these niggaz. That's part of the deal I am signing with the Duffel Bag Cartel, and the homie Taurus."

Kim-Kim stood in front of him. "Well, aren't you just special?"

"Ain't got shit into do wit' being special. It's about money and a whole lot of that shit." Preston puffed on his blunt. "Any way I can make a bunch of cash I'm on that shit. But that's needless to say. For the record, read yo' contract, you signed to Bread Gang, but I get fifty-one percent of everything. The God gets paid before them niggaz do." He laughed.

Kayley came over and sat on his lap. "Damn, baby, you bussing her head left and right. Take it easy, she is still my sister you know." Kayley kissed his cheek.

Preston rubbed her thick thighs. She was also wearing a one-piece Fendi swimsuit. "Ain't nothing personal, it's just business."

Kim-Kim came and kneeled on the side of him. She kissed his cheek. "I'm saying, I ain't know what I was signing. So, what does it mean? Does it mean that I don't get no money?"

"N'all, shorty, just means that I own you as an artist. You belong to the Cutthroat Mafia more than you do the Bread Gang," Preston explained.

Kim-Kim rubbed his stomach. He had on a Polo button-up that was wide open. "Guess I don't mind being owned by you as long as Kayley really is the one running the show." She looked up at Kayley.

Kayley smiled. "You better know it."

Kim-Kim grinned. "Say, sis, I heard mama wit' him a few times already. And well, you know I ain't got no ol' man kinda cause I don't trust none of those men in Harris County. But whatta you say to let me get a go at Preston. You know since I belong to him and y'all gon' be leaving real soon and thangs. To be honest I wanna see how it feels for him to slide deep inside of me. Kinda want him to fuck me like he did mama, and you. I've fingered myself enough listening and peeking on y'all sessions." She squeezed Preston's dick. "How 'bout it sis?"

Kayley looked out to the water. "Kim-Kim why should I let you fuck my man? What kind of value would he have to me if I did such a thang?"

Kim-Kim shrugged her shoulders. "A whole lot if you ask me. Don't mean that you don't value him a nothin' if you let him fuck yo sister. We keep everythang in the family anyway. Even when you and I were little girls we did some thangs together that still makes me tremble. First and only time I tasted some kitty came from between your legs."

Kayley blushed. "Girl shut yo old trap. Always gotta be bumping those big old lips. Some thangs ain't meant to be exposed."

Preston moved Kayley off his lap a bit more and groaned when he felt Kim-Kim squeeze his dick in her hand. "Aw hell n'all, she done said too much now. Go head on. What are you talking about?"

Kim-Kim smiled and licked her lips. "Well, when we were little, Kayley here was a straight freak."

She looked up at Kayley. "That coochie between her thighs used to stay on fire. She had a habit of climbing into my bed in the middle of the night, grabbing my hand and putting it between her legs. She'd wrap her thighs around it and grinded for a while before she forced me to put it inside of her panties."

"Kim-Kim, I swear to God if you don't shut up, I'm about to whoop yo' silly ass. Now shut up!" Kayley snapped.

Kim-Kim smiled. "Whatever, I don't know why you are so self-conscious about it now anyway. It's like who cares. So, what, we used to experiment when we were little girls, who didn't?" She squeezed Preston's dick harder. "And clearly it ain't affecting your man in a negative way. His shit jumping like crazy." She stuck her head into his lap some more and tried to smell his piece through his pants.

Kayley hopped up and pushed Kim-Kim off Preston. "Bitch ain't nothing happening. This my man. You gotta find yo' own. Come on, Preston, I need you to step inside the cabin for a minute so you and I can holler." She rolled her eyes at Kim-Kim as Preston stood with his dick poked out in front of him.

Kim-Kim stood up and crossed her arms. "Aw, I see how it is. Y'all invite me out here on this Yacht and then kick me to the curb. This is just wrong!" she snapped, but it was too late, the pair disappeared into the cabin.

Ghost

Chapter 14

It was day eleven, and Lashawn was starting to feel stronger. She occasionally had episodes where she became nauseous and even vomited or others where she suffered from violent busy spasms. For the most part, she was doing better, and true to his word, Macho had not left her side. He called shots from his home and whenever he absolutely was forced to leave the house to attend to business, he took Lashawn along with him. As the days wore on Lashawn became less defiant and more susceptible to his love and care. Macho handled her as gently as a savage could. He was patient, understanding, and forgiving when he needed to be.

By day twenty- two Lashawn was showing promise. Her face began to put some of its weight back on, and she was eating regularly, even though, her system had an extremely difficult time keeping everything down. Macho tended to her around the clock. He bathed her himself, he fed her, he massaged her, he held her, and he worshipped her by bowing in front of her and letting her know how much she meant to him.

The only thing he didn't do was sleep with her from fear of what she may have contracted during her period of weakness. Though Macho loved her, he had no sexual desire toward her because of George and he hated himself for losing interest within the most beautiful and precious woman he felt he had ever seen in his entire life.

On the twenty-fifth day, he and Lashawn were laying in the bed on their sides. She was in front of him before she turned all the way around to look him into his eyes. She reached out to hold his face. The sun had just set outside, and there was a cool breeze coming from the open window of the bedroom.

"Macho, are you sickened by me now?" Her breath smelled like spearmint gum.

Macho frowned and looked into her eyes. "What are you talking about?"

Lashawn continued to search his eyes. "We've been together every single day for the past twenty-five days and you haven't made one pass at me. Before, you used to be all over me. All you thought about was sex whenever you saw me, and you tried me every time you and I were alone. I noticed the change. I can't really fault you for feeling how you feel. I just gotta know honestly, are you turned off by me now?"

Macho took a deep breath and exhaled. "You're my heart, Lashawn. I love the fuck out of you."

"But?"

"But seeing as that nigga George clapped you I can't help but worry about what disease he gave you. Kid be all through Baltimore slaying those junkie broads. Nine times out of ten he gave you somethin' and I ain't trying to catch it."

Lashawn nodded for a moment. She slowly sat up and exhaled. "I figured it was something. I guess this whole time that I was thinking things were going to take a positive turn between you and me, was all in my head. God, Macho, what do you want me to do? You want me to get tested?"

Macho slid out the bed. "Of course, but I ain't trying to force shit up on you, right now. My main thang is that you kick that heroin habit. Sex ain't that important. I'm good."

"Now you're good? Wow." She ran her fingers through her hair. "You know what, let's go." She walked to the closet and threw open the door.

"Let's go where? We ain't finna go nowhere." Macho stepped over to her.

Lashawn dropped her gown and began getting dressed. "Yes, the fuck we are. You're about to take me to the hospital, and I'm going to get tested for every disease out including that Covid-19 shit. Once my results come back that I am clean we should be able to move on with our lives. I don't like feeling that you're repulsed by me. I demand to be desired, and if I am tired of being desired, I still want you to get on my nerves about the whole sex thing. It's a woman's place to tell a man that he's doing too much, and to ask him if sex is all that he thinks about when it comes to her. I miss that option. So, let's go."

Macho started to get ready. "Are you serious, right now?" He was with it because he was tired of worrying about the subject. He wanted to know once and for all, what she had if anything at all.

"I'm very serious, and I think that while I am getting checked for everything, you should too."

Macho shrugged his shoulders. "Shit, why not? I'm wit' it."

"Good then, we both wit' it, so let's rollout." Lashawn grabbed her purse, cellphone, and bottled water before heading out of the room with a look of determination. She wanted to get it all over and done with, and so did Macho.

***

George sat in front of the detective shaking like a leaf. He took a long pull off the Newport cigarette and blew the smoke to the ceiling. "I done told y'all everything that took place on the night of the robbery. Now, what happens?"

Detective Wilson was a bald, physically fit, white man with serious eyes and a permanent mug on his face. He sipped from his black coffee. "You wanna tell me why you managed to keep this from us for a full year?"

George shrugged his shoulders. "I thought my brother might kill me. He crazy, and his homeboy is too. They run this gang called the Cutthroat Mafia. They killed up a bunch of rivals that run under that damn boy Burleigh too. In fact, a bitch from their crew is the one that killed Burleigh. They some mean son of a bitchez. That's why I was scared to say anything. You gotta understand man."

Detective Wilson frowned. "Boy, what are you talking about? You saying that your brother and his crew are responsible for killings that took place in Baltimore? How so?"

"Damn, Pig, you not listening to me. My brother is Macho James. His right-hand man's name is Preston Miller. They are the leaders of the Cutthroat Mafia. They sell heroin, cocaine, exotic strands of weed, guns, and they murder muthafuckas like Raid kill roaches, n'all scratch that, better than Raid. Now you wanted me to snitch earlier and I couldn't have cause they woulda chopped me up like they did Burleigh's body. These boys are dangerous. You see what Macho did to the back of my head. He hit me wit' a golf club right nasty if I might say so myself. If y'all don't get him and his crazy ass homeboy off the street they gon' take over this city in blood."

Detective Wilson rubbed his chin. He looked across the interrogation table at George and didn't know whether to take him seriously or not. "George James, if you're telling me the truth this is above my pay grade. I need to make a few phone calls. You sit tight. Smoke as many cigarettes as you like."

"Say, man, whoever you finna call, tell them that I don't work for free. There is a price for my information and I'ma need some protection, too. Don't forget Swine." He pointed at him and crossed his skinny legs, taking another cigarette out of the pack, and sparking it.

"Yeah, sure, I got you. Compensation, go figure." He closed the door and left the room.

***

It had been six full hours before Lashawn was called to be seen. The hospital was near its capacity from dealing with Covid-19 patients. Because the nurse behind the desk made both Lashawn and Macho fill out their paperwork separately, and Lashawn finished first she was called first. As she was going into her room to see the doctor and nurse, Macho's phone rang. He held up one finger to Lashawn and went into the bathroom while she was led to her room. As soon as he placed the phone to his ear his top security hitta started to talk.

"Yo', boss, we got about eighty Philly niggaz on Colgate demanding to see you. The leader of these niggaz, some cat named Kilroy says he runs the Rotten To The Core Mafia, and he personally needs to speak with you before a war breaks out. What do you want me to do?"

Macho was already clenching his jaw with a scowl on his face. "Tell that nigga I'll be there in thirty minutes." He hung up. "Bitch ass niggaz come all the way from Philly this deep? Fuck they on?" He called Angela. "Yo', Shorty, who the fuck is Kilroy?"

Angela mugged her phone. "Thanks for asking how I'm doing first, Macho. And why haven't you returned any of my texts or messages?"

"Yo', miss the God wit' that bullshit. Who is Kilroy?"

Angela sighed. "The only Kilroy I know is from Philly. Why are you inquiring about him?"

Macho was getting heated. "Because bitch, that nigga and seventy-nine other niggaz is on Colgate right now asking for the don. Somethin' ain't right. Fuck am I walking into?"

Angela wracked her brain. "Holy shit, he knows."

Macho mugged his phone. "Excuse you."

"Macho, he knows that you were coming from North Philly and Kensington Park. Just like we are high up in the game we have rivals, and our rival's job is to figure out what we are doing and to put a stop to it. Kilroy knows and this is going to be the calm before the storm. United States and Russia."

Macho was confused. "Bitch, what?"

"Two superpowers going at each other unless there is a treaty. I'm in Australia right now but I fly back in three days. Tell him what he needs to hear until then, and we'll go from there."

Macho took the phone off his ear. "Bitch, this nigga came to Baltimore. This is my homeland. Fuck what he wanna hear. Nigga want that smoke then he gotta prepare to choke." He hung up the phone and went out to the nurse's station and told them to tell Lashawn that something important came up. Her ride was outside, and to be smart. That he loved her. The nurse wrote down the message and he bounced.

***

Preston stood in the middle of the graveyard as the wind picked up its velocity and caused his Chanel fit to blow in the wind. Phoenix stepped next to him and wrapped his arm around his neck. "Say, Mane, one thang 'bout the game is that it is exactly what its name says that it is. A fucking game." He drank from his bottle of Hennessey.

Preston didn't like any man putting his arm around his neck. He didn't like the closeness. "Yo', Dunn, why the fuck are we in a graveyard, right now?"

"When you ain't got no money or shit that's when two homeboys are the closest. But when the money comes, so does the bitchez. Then the haters, and that's when the problems come in. When two niggaz enter the game at the same time the streets always pick which one of the two they want to see as the true leader. Even the enemies pick the true king."

"Nigga, what?"

Phoenix stepped away from him and stood over the tombstone. "Today is Mikey's birthday. Son of a bitch woulda been thirty-nine just like me." He drank from his bottle. "But he ain't cause he dead." He snickered.

Preston looked down at the tombstone. "Who the fuck is Mikey?"

Phoenix took another swallow from his bottle. "Mikey was my right-hand man, and the only killa I ever loved outside of Taurus. Me and that nigga went through everythang together, before he had to be crushed." Phoenix mugged Mikey's tombstone.

Preston watched him closely. "Yo', if that was ya mans, why you crush him? And once again why did you bring me here?"

Phoenix kept staring at the tombstone. "Say, Mane, another thang 'bout the game is that it doesn't allow right-hand men or friends to remain friends. The game will give you a whole lot of money. A whole lot of bitchez, but never any happiness, well, not that's long term anyway." He drank from the Hennessey again, finished it, and threw the bottle at full speed against the tombstone. It exploded.

Preston was popped into the face with some of the glass, but he didn't move. "You still ain't answered my question."

Phoenix kneeled and ran his fingers over the lettering of Mikey's headstone. "I crushed this nigga because there could only be one king of the Duffel Bag Cartel. True kings stand alone. We started out as equals, but the game took us down a highway of a bunch of shit that separated all that emotional shit. When it's all said and done a boss ain't got no partner.

Not when it's the same mob." He smiled. "That nigga made a few plays on my life. The game ain't nothing but Chess. Check muthafuckin' mate, Mikey."

Preston came over and squatted down beside him. "Now that you explained that. Tell me why you brought me here."

"This ain't nothing but your future. Before it's all said and done, you're either going to be the one laying in a coffin while Macho reigns supreme or Macho's going to be the one in the dirt and you'll be standing over his grave every birthday. Either way, the Duffel Bag Cartel can only support one leader, and we choosing you. I don't give a fuck if Macho do got our blood in him. Fuck the nepotism."

Preston stood up. "Hold up, you saying that you some kin to Macho? How?"

Phoenix sucked his teeth. "That shit doesn't even matter. Just get yo shit together wit' me before you leave. You gon' have everything that you need. Take care of Kayley and you'll never have shit to worry about. Keep your bitch close, and your money even closer. Trust no man or no bitch. Make it all about the cash. Best advice I can give you, young nigga." He wiped some brush off Mikey's grave. "Contrary to what you may think, Preston, I loved Mikey. That nigga was my heart. We murdered niggaz together, fucked hoez together, and ran up a check. In the end, the game just always wins." He patted him on the back. "Like I said, though, hit me up before you leave and we gon' get everything in order and set shit in motion. A'ight? Let's roll Mane."

"A'ight." Preston stared at Mikey's grave for a little while longer before he got back into Phoenix's Rolls Royce and pulled out of the cemetery with ten trucks filled with the Duffel Bag Cartel surrounding them on security.

Chapter 15

On the night before Preston left Houston Kayley woke him up at two in the morning saying that her father wanted to see her before she left. That it was important, and that she didn't have a choice in the matter so she left. It took Preston thirty full minutes before he dozed back off to sleep snoring lightly. An hour later he awoke to the sounds of the bedsprings squeaking loudly. When he opened his eyes, he saw Kim-Kim crawling across the bed in a short purple négligee. Her breasts were plump and jiggling. She didn't stop crawling across the bed until she was straddling his lap.

"Well, Preston, I was thinking. You're leaving tomorrow and it seems dat I'm da only one in dis house that ain't got a chance to see what dis here dick 'bout. I'm thinking dat it ain't fair. So, what do you say we fix all dat fo my sister get back here and break up da party?" She took a hold of his waistband and slowly pulled it down his big muscular thighs. When his dick sprung up, she grabbed it, beating it in her hand. "Damn, this is a whole lot of meat right here, Playboy. See why my mama and my sister was hollering like you was killing dem." She pulled the skin back and licked around the head moaning and sucking it partway into her mouth.

Preston was slowly waking up out of his daze. He spaced his thighs and groaned. Kim-Kim sucked him harder and harder. "Mmm. Mmm. Kim-Kim, damn bitch, you sucking my dick."

She spit on the tip of it and slurped it down the entire pipe, then pulled it out only to suck it back down again. Then her face was going haywire in his lap. She sucked like a pro while she kneeled over his lap on all fours with her negligée around her waist.

Preston slapped her ass and ran his fingers in between the cheeks playing with her crinkle back there. "You so strapped lil' sis. I wanna hit this ass. When a bitch this thick you gotta fuck that ass. What you think 'bout that?"

She took her mouth off his dick and licked around it. "I'm yo' sister. You the boy, we can do whatever you wanna do." Her face disappeared in his lap.

Preston grabbed a handful of her hair and guided it into his lap over and over. He smacked her ass again and gripped the booty meat there. He pulled her closer to him. He sucked his finger and slipped it into her ring. "I'm finna fuck dis ass. You my mafuckin' lil' sister."

Kim-Kim sucked faster and faster. "Shut up, Preston. That shit do somethin' to me when you say dat shit."

"Suck that pipe, sis. Swallow that mafuckas den let me fuck this ass."

Kim-Kim screeched and sucked hard and fast with no hands. Her jaws hollowed in and out. She added spit. She moaned loudly and breathed heavily through her nose.

Preston pulled his dick back before he came. He didn't want to waste his nut. He brutally threw her on her stomach and fell on top of her opening her ass. He spit right on her anus, and fingered it, getting her nice and wet. Then he spit again, and it landed in the same spot. He pushed her right thick thigh to her ribs, and slowly worked his way into her ass.

Kim-Kim clawed at the bed. She grabbed a handful of the sheets. "Uhhh, big bruh. You finna fuck me back there, ain't you? Ohhh, shit."

Preston was beyond the talking. He guided his dick into her and slammed it home. She groaned. He pulled her up until she was on all fours again. Once there he proceeded to fuck her like a horse holding on to her hips. He slapped her thick ass cheeks.

Smack!

"Uhhh! Shit!" Kim-Kim laid her head on the pillow for a second, then she grabbed it and bit into it screaming at the top of her lungs. Her ass spread. She felt like he was stuffing her. Her pussy dripped her fluids.

Smack! Smack! Smack! Smack!

Preston drove into her faster and faster, stroking her. "Gimme this ass, bitch. Gimme this shit!" he growled.

Smack! Smack! Smack! Smack!

His hand crashed into her ass against and again. She moaned louder with her mouth wide open. Preston felt between her thighs. He rubbed in between her sex lips while he pulled back. Two fingers dived deep into her pussy. "Yo, I gotta wax this pussy, too. I'd be a damn fool if I didn't." He pulled out of her ass and sucked her pussy from behind while his piece rubbed along the length of the bedsheets.

Kim-Kim gripped the sheets and moaned loudly with her back arched. She looked over her shoulders for a moment to see his face stuffed into her middle. She could hear the loud sucking and the audio drove her crazy. "You gon' make me cum, Preston. I swear to God you gon' make me cum."

Preston flicked her clitoris firmly at full speed. He trapped it with his lips and sucked hard. She screamed and came shaking out of control. Preston got back to his knees and slid into her ass again. Now he was really fucking her with no mercy. Her big booty slammed into his stomach over and over. He slapped the sides of it and squeezed the flesh. He shivered, and came hard, pulling out and bussing all over her cheeks in thick ropes.

Kim-Kim moaned. She turned around, took a hold of it, and pumped it as fast as she could while he came all over her neck, and titties. Then she pushed him down, grabbed a wet wipe off the nightstand, wiped his dick off, and slid on to it.

"You finna fuck this pussy, nigga." She sank down on him with her eyes rolling to the back of his head. Her ass popped over and over. Uhhh! Uhhhh! Uhhhh! Fuck! Fuck me! Fuck me, awwww shit baby!"

Preston opened her négligée and sucked her breasts one at a time. Her hips popped, and back curled, she worked him, bouncing up and down on top of him. Their scents rose into the air. It fueled Kim-Kim to go harder. She leaned down and sucked his neck just as his fingers went into her ass again, and she came screaming.

Preston allowed her to shake for a full minute before flipped her over and got between her thighs pounding away. "Dis. What. You. Hoez. Needed?" *Bam! Bam! Bam! Bam!* "If. I. Grew. Up. Wit. Y'all. Ass. I woulda been fucking all three of you every single day." *Bam! Bam! Bam!* "I wouldn't care what y'all was to meeeee! Shit!" He dug deeper and felt his body trembling.

Kim-Kim threw her thighs wide open. "Awww fuck! Fuck! I'm cummminggg you nasty ass nigga! Uh, I wish you grew up wit' usssss! Uhhhhh!" she screamed.

Preston pushed her into a ball and fucked her as fast and as hard as he could until he started to cum. "I'm cumming sis, shit I'm cumming." He jerked and kept diving into her while he kept her pushed into a ball.

***

"I shoulda known that my father wasn't calling me, Phoenix. He doesn't ever use my phone when he needs to get in touch with me, he just shows up. Damn, I'm so stupid." Kayley shook her head and lowered it.

Phoenix walked up on her inside of his three-story mansion and forced her to the wall. He took his right hand and slid it under her short Gucci skirt. He rubbed her pussy over her satin red panties. "I'm saying, though. How the fuck my cuz gon' come through Harris county and not make a pit stop for old time's sake? Whatever since you and Taurus got back in tune you feeling like we don't do what our family does no more?" He pushed the panties into her coochie and rubbed the soft plump lips.

Kayley shivered. "Phoenix, it ain't nothing like that and you know it. I was just trying to chill. I thought we said it wasn't going to be no more fuckin' going on inside of the family, I mean besides you and Natalia. Whatever happened to that?"

Phoenix kissed her neck. "I ain't never said nothing like that. I am who I am. I prefer our pussy over other pussy. Your father tends to be the same way for the most part, and you are, too. Out of all his daughters, you got to be one of the finest, damn." He gripped her juicy booty and bit into her neck. Seconds later his hand was going into her panties feeling her naked pussy.

"I bet if my sister heard you say that she'd gut you like a fish." She spoke in reference of Natalia but didn't bother to take his hand out of her panties.

Phoenix separated her pussy lips and slipped two fingers up her box. "You still daddy's little girl? Or do you belong to cuz like you used, too?" He began to finger her deeper and deeper.

"I don't belong to nobody but me, unnnn. S-s-s-stop." Her eyes closed.

Phoenix kissed her lips and licked them. "You got on these see-through panties and thongs. You must've thought Taurus was calling you. You thought he was gon' fuck this pussy, didn't you?"

Kayley moaned. "Shut up. That's my daddy. Why are you talking like that?"

Phoenix fingered deeper. "You don't think I know he fuckin' you." Faster with his fingering, deeper and deeper. His digit was dripping with her essence. "I know he been fuckin' yo thick ass. I know how our family gets down. Taurus would be a fool to not fuck his thickest shawty." He picked her up and fell to the floor with her. He slipped his finger back into her and kept it moving. "Tell the truth." His thumb rolled all over her clitoris.

Kayley held her thighs wide open humping into his finger. "Stop. Stop. Ohhhh, please cuz, stop playin' wit my pussy. You ain't right."

Phoenix leaned his face down and sniffed her box. He sucked on her pearl while he fingered her at full speed. She squirmed around on the floor and whimpered. "Tell me you want daddy to fuck this pussy. Say it lil' cuz. Feel that blood coursing through yo ass, don't fight it. Tell the truth. He been fuckin' you, ain't he?"

Kayley screamed she was close to cumming. "Shut up, he ain't never touched me. Uhhh! Uhhh! Uhhh!" Her thighs opened further.

"Tell the truth! Tell me, he been fuckin' yo thick ass?" Phoenix's fingers were a blur going in and out of her.

Her juices formed a puddle under her ass. She was humping upward and imagining some of the most taboo visions that she could envision. She raised her knees and came hard with Phoenix pinching her clitoris. "Awwww, shiiitttt cuz, you so bogus! You so bogus!"

Phoenix kept sucking on her pearl until she stopped quivering. Then he climbed between her thighs and slipped into her pussy slamming deep. "Uhhhh!" he groaned. "Back in this pussy." He began to drive in and out clapping his middle into hers.

Kayley pushed at his chest for a moment, then she wrapped her thighs around his waist and allowed him to long stroke her while she arched her back and moaned at the top of her lungs. The feeling kept getting better and better. "Uh! Uh! Uh! Why Phoenix? Why? Why my pussy. You wit' my sister?"

Phoenix pulled her closer to him and really began to slam home. She was so wet that he could feel her dripping off his balls. "You my family." Harder and harder he stabbed, rolling his back. "You fuckin' that nigga. He ain't no kin to us." He leaned down and sucked all over her lips.

Kayley darted her tongue out at him. She wrapped her arms around his neck and pulled him down further. "Why, why, why? Uhhhh! Why I can't break the cycle. Uh! Uh! Uh! Phoenix, why can't I fuck somebody outside of our-uhhhh!"

Phoenix bit into her neck and fucked her so hard that all she could do was scream with her mouth wide open. He felt her cumming. He flipped her onto her knees and slid back into her horse style going in and out of her pussy at full speed. Their skins slapped into each other's. Their scents wafted into the air. It was forbidden sex at its finest. Phoenix rubbed her fat ass.

"You belong to this family! We get this pussy first!" He pushed her to the ground on her stomach and laid on top of her stroking away. She moved her right knee to her rib cage moaning so loud that it sounded like she was being killed by an attacker. Phoenix rubbed her thick thigh while he dug her out. "Cum for me, cuz. Cum for me!" He licked into her earlobe.

Kayley threw her head back and groaned. The tremors rushed all over her body. She forced her eyes closed and whimpered. She hated herself for cheating on Preston. She loved him so much. They were made for each other. She didn't know how she was going to look him in the eyes when she got back to Jackie's place. She figured she would cross that bridge when she got to it. She felt Phoenix slid his two fingers into her back door. She screamed and came panting at the top of her lungs.

Phoenix plunged and plunged. He pulled her ass all the way back into his lap and came back to back. His dick was dripping with her secretions. He pulled it out and fed it to her. Kayley sucked with no inhibitions. Her forbidden blood coursing through her red hot now. She sucked and sucked tasting the remnants of their mixture and it drove her crazy. When she was sure that there was no more milking to be done, she laid on her back with her thighs wide open. Phoenix laid beside her playing with her pussy. "I don't know why Taurus daughters got the best pussy, but damn y'all do. Every time I get to fiendin' for this shit I'm coming to get me some of it. You are a Stevens. I don't give a fuck who you wit' never forget that shit." He leaned down and they began to make out loudly for five minutes. When Phoenix broke the kiss, Kayley was breathing hard.

Phoenix sat up. "A'ight, now let me tell you how we finna use this nigga to get the Duffel Bag Cartel to where it needs to be. Your role is important, so listen up." He cupped her pussy and rubbed it while he put her up on game.

Chapter 16

It was just past midnight when Macho sped down the block rolling his black Benz truck with ten other trucks behind him filled with savages from his Cutthroat Mafia. He was able to spot Kilroy and his crew of Philly hittas as soon as he turned the corner onto Colgate Avenue. They stood in the middle of the street blocking it off. This caused Macho to frown his face in anger. He grabbed his Mach-90 from under his seat and placed it on his lap. His truck was full of Cutthroat Mafia members as well. All around his truck was the sound of assault rifles being cocked and loaded.

When Macho got to the group of Philly invaders he slammed on his brakes and threw his truck in park. In seconds he had the driver's door open jumping out of it with a red rag around his neck. Behind him, his killas had their red rags with Cutthroat printed on them in black pulped over their faces. They followed Macho. Macho walked right through the crowd of armed Philly hittas and stopped in front of Kilroy.

Kilroy was five-feet-ten inches tall, dark-skinned, with a face like that rapper Biggie Smalls. He was bald and wore Chanel sunglasses over his eyes. He was short-tempered and had more than fifty bodies under his belt. They referred to him in Philadelphia as the Black Reaper. He was head of the Rotten To The Core mafia.

"Fuck the bidness is, nigga? Why you all in blood hood deep like this? You niggaz want war a somethin'?" Macho snapped. "This Cutthroat Pa'." He was riled up and ready to blast, Kilroy.

Kilroy mugged him and laughed. "Yo', son, you mean to tell me you're Macho?" He pointed at him with his thumb and looked over his shoulder at his Rotten To The Core mob before he was back mugging Macho.

"Yeah, nigga, Macho James. Mr. B-more. What it do?" Macho stepped closer.

Six of Kilroy's troops rolled up on Ducattis and got off their bikes with black helmets over their heads and guns in both hands. Kilroy took his glasses off. There was a small scar under his right eye, and five teardrops under his left one.

"Word on the street is that the Cutthroat mafia is coming for Kensington Park and North Philly. Seeing as that's the word, and you're the leader of the Cutthroat Mafia I thought it was in my best interest to roll out here to let you know that first off shit ain't sweet, and secondly if you so much as step anywhere near Philly I'ma be forced to break that shit up as only I know how. We from Philly, son. We a whole different breed of killa, trust me when I tell you that B."

"Yeah, well, dis is Baltimore Pa. We don't give a fuck about you Philly niggaz. In this city, I run this bitch. My niggaz eat whatever I put on the menu, and we fucks wit' a variety like buffets. We got this shit sewed up here like Tailor shops. Now far as Philly goes, if I wanted to make that transition, I woulda done it already. Ain't no hoez over here Blood, word to Dundalk on back."

Kilroy laughed. "Yousa clown." He wiped his mouth. "I really don't do this whole standoff shit. I'm 'bout that pistol popping, body dropping shit. I came to see what the fuck you niggaz wanna do. We right here, Philly is in the neighborhood. You wanna invade my shit, drop me right here son. Or else stay the fuck outta my land, this is your final warning."

"*Warning,* nigga fuck yo' warning, and fuck Philly. You mafuckas ain't on shit wit' the city. What?" Macho was ready to get it lit. After saying that, ten more trucks filled with the Cutthroat Mafia rolled up and unloaded with assault rifles in their hands. They stood behind Macho ready for his command to react and crush the Rotten To The Core Mafia.

Kilroy eyed him with extreme hatred. "Yeah, Macho, I guess you are a bit deeper than me now, ain't you? Good thang numbers don't mean shit unless they coming from a money machine." He pulled his nose.

Macho stepped in his face. "Get the fuck out of Baltimore my nigga. This yo' final warning. If I catch wind that you are still in my city by morning, word to God I'm coming to exterminate you niggaz. From this day forth we got a problem with you Philly niggaz. And when I say it's a problem, it's a *major* fuckin' problem for everybody that I'm feeding. You fuck niggaz just got put on the menu. Now step or get stomped out. Fuck you wanna do?" Macho took a step back and raised his right hand.

Red beams from his crew landed on every Philly member. There were Shooters in the trees that Kilroy hadn't spotted until they enacted their red beams. Shooters from attic windows, and Shooters from bushes that placed their beams all over Kilroy's face and neck.

Macho laughed a murderous laugh. "This what that B-more shit look like kid, word the fuck up. Bounce!"

Kilroy lowered his eyes. "Yeah, Macho, you got it, Dunn." He nodded and stepped forward. "That beef shit is in my heart. I don't lose at it. This shit ain't over kid. I'm a Philly nigga, we don't take Ls. I promise you that, but round one, you. You got it." He eyed Macho's crew of savages. "Yeah, Macho, you got it this time. We out!" He turned around and jumped in his Range Rover truck storming down the street banging *Meek Mill's Stuck In My Ways.*

Macho watched his broken lights for a long time before he turned around and began to shake up with his crew. "Yo', steak and egg breakfasts for everybody in the morning, word up. Cutthroat!"

"Gang! Gang!" His crew yelled.

"Cutthroat!" He hollered with his right hand acting as bull horn.

"Gang, gang!" His crew hollered back.

"Whose city?" Macho roared.

"Cutthroat!" They answered.

"Gang, gang," Macho responded. His chest heaved up and down from the excitement.

***

Detective Wilson and Federal Agent Walker sat in Walker's all-black Cadillac Escalade taking notes. They snapped pictures and recorded as much of the malarkey as they could. Detective Wilson shook his head. "Yeah, this is well above my pay grade. I guess it'll be wise for us to hand this investigation over to the united states government." He sighed in defeat.

Agent Walker had ten years logged in with the department of justice. He was an Italian man with wavy hair and a handsome face. He looked over to Wilson and smiled. "Wilson if the state wanted to keep this case they couldn't. That man that just rolled off, his name is Kilroy Stevens. He is one of the deadliest mobsters on the east coast. He specializes in murder, extortion, firearms, and narcotics. I don't know who pissed him off, but now that he's stepped foot in Baltimore you boys have a problem." He laughed. "I guarantee the murder rate increases. Yeah, I am curious to see how this unfolds. Besides, ain't your department getting defunded?" He pulled away from the curb with a sneer on his face.

"Fuck off. Drop me back off at the station so I can log in this data. You're such a dick." Wilson frowned at him. "We still get the Burleigh murder and the hold-up off the Arab stores and any other murders we can find that reports back to this Cutthroat Mafia. Deal?"

Walker smiled. "You get the trash left behind? You know how this goes. Now shut up and thank God that some real law enforcement has signed on to help this faltering city. Lord knows you needed the help." Walker turned up the radio to a Garth Brooks song and began to sing along ignoring Wilson for the rest of the ride.

He had some things in mind for Macho and his crew, and he hoped the result would amount to life in Federal prison. If he could indict fifty of the Cutthroat Mafia members, he could be shot up the ladder right into the Pentagon. That was his ultimate goal. He had to be careful, though. He was aware that Kilroy and the Rotten To The Core crew were already being secretly indicted. Their investigation was sensitive and highly important to the United States government. He needed to pull some strings, but in the end, he would get what he was asking for. He was sure of it.

***

When Kayley got back to her mother's home that night she found Preston up watching a repeated Laker's game. He looked back at her and got out of the bed pulling her into his embrace. "Hey, baby, what did yo pops want?"

Kayley could feel Phoenix's cum running down her inner thighs. "He didn't want me, Phoenix did. We just kicked it at his mansion and talked business. What are you still doing up?" She scanned the room and eased out of his embrace. She walked to the dresser and picked out some clothes so she could get into the shower.

Preston eyed her suspiciously. "I was watching LeBron. I missed the game earlier but they playing it again. You already know that every game counts because of this Coronavirus shit. I can't miss my nigga making history. Fuck Phoenix have you lie to me for, though?"

Kayley looked over her shoulder at him while she grabbed a pair of panties out of the top dresser drawer. "Who says that Phoenix told me to lie to you? I never said that." She gathered the clothes into her arms and grabbed a body towel to wash up with. She felt Phoenix's semen slid down her inner thighs and onto her ankle. She felt so uncomfortable, and nasty.

"Yo, well, if he ain't tell you to lie to me then you shoulda called and told me that you were with him instead of your old man. Simple communication, that's all I'm asking for."

Kayley eyed him from the mirror. "Oh, so now you call yourself getting all clingy and shit? Since when nigga?"

"Since right now. It's the middle of the night and you just bringing yo' ass back into the crib. I ain't from Houston. I don't know how many mafuckas you know down here, but I can only guess. Far as I know you could of went to meet up with one of your old niggaz or somethin'." He sat on the bed and continued watching the Laker's game.

Kayley continued to look him over from the mirror. Suddenly she felt very guilty about what she'd just done with Phoenix. She never wanted to be deceitful or evil toward Preston. She was sure that she loved him. She turned around to face him. "Baby, I'm sorry." Phoenix's cum slid down to her foot and oozed to the sole of the right one.

"You good, Shorty. I ain't mean to be jocking you on some stalker type shit. You was with yo' cousin, it's good." He sat back and turned the game up a bit.

Kayley sighed. "Well, I was with Phoenix. Just him. I wasn't messing around with no old boyfriends or anything like that, so you don't have to worry about that. Besides, I love

136

you, baby. Don't you trust me?" She sat on the edge of the bed.

Preston nodded. "Yeah, I do. Now gon' in there and wash yo ass. You smell some type of way," he joked.

Kayley stood up embarrassed. "You fa real?"

Preston held his nose. "Damn, bitch," once again just joking.

Kayley avoided his eyes. "Yeah, let me handle dis bidness and I'ma get in the bed. I'll be out in an hour." She eased into the bathroom and closed the door.

Preston had seen the bite marks on her neck, and the gel-like fluid that oozed down her thighs. He knew that she'd been somewhere and with somebody, but he wasn't sweating it. Not after all of the things that he and Kim-Kim had done in Kayley's absence. He got up out of the bed and placed his ear to the bathroom door. He waited until he heard the water running before he made haste to Kim-Kim's bedroom. He found her laying on her back with her thighs wide open.

She had an eight-inch fan situated so that it was blowing right on her pussy to cool it down. Preston crept into the room and kneeled on the bed. He lowered his face between her thighs and sucked her pussy lips into his mouth moaning in the back of his throat. She opened them wider under the pretense of being asleep. He spread her sex lips and licked up and down her slit until she came all over his chin, then he slipped back out of the room and walked past the bathroom door, mugging it.

Ghost

Chapter 17

"So now that you know I don't have anything, can you begin to look at me differently? And will you stop making me feel like I should be ostracized because of the wrong choices that I made while I was at my lowest point in life?" Lashawn asked as she sat across the kitchen table from Macho.

She'd spent all afternoon making dinner that consisted of fried chicken, brown rice, pinto beans, cornbread, collard greens, yams, and a 7-Up pound cake with glaze. She was celebrating the fact that she was disease-free. However, she didn't know how to tell him the other news of her being pregnant. She chose to fight one battle at a time.

Macho ripped his chicken from the bone like a savage. It was drenched in Louisiana hot sauce and was fire to him. "Yo', I ain't never intended to make you feel like nothing more than a queen. I got mad love and admiration for you and I just wanna see the best for you that's all." He continued to eat his food. "You being healthy is defined, but what's up, though. I still feel like I need to take a good look at George. I feel like that nigga wanted to fuck you just to get back at me. Niggaz be doing that type of shit all the time."

"Girls do, too. That's why I ain't got no friends now." Lashawn forked up a bit of collard greens that were soaked in hot sauce and cornbread.

"You sho' that's the reason you ain't got no friends?" Macho laughed.

Lashawn glared at him. "Stop playin' wit' me, Macho."

"Aw baby." He wiped his mouth on a napkin and stood up taking a hold of her hand. He guided her into the living room and turned on the laptop and in seconds had *Trey Songz's Reflection* bellowing out of the speakers. He held her close to his body. Took her hand and interlocked his fingers with hers.

He kissed her cheek. "Yo,' Shawn, I've been crazy about you since day one shorty, no cap." He kissed her cheek. "Ever since the homie introduced you as his sister."

Lashawn smiled. "Yeah, and on the low, I was feeling you just as much as you were feeling me. I just didn't act on my urges because I was going through so much back then. Pooh had me mentally all over the place. Then I was dealing with severe bouts of depression. Sometimes, I get so low that the only viable option seems to be suicide. I try my best to shake off that feeling but when it comes, it's worse than a bitch on her period."

Macho held her closer. "I ain't even know that you suffered from depression."

"Yeah, I do. It seems to run on my father's side of the family real tough. Guess his apple didn't fall too far from the tree." She kept dancing and looked up at him. "I got a lot of problems, don't I?"

Macho laughed. "Shorty you good. Shit, I might not have depression and all that shit but I'm fucked up, too. I think when you come from where we come from. And you are forced to endure the things that we do on a daily basis. Things that the world deems as *normal* for our people to endure, you're bound to suffer from somethin'."

Lashawn nodded agreeing. "Yeah, well, I already told you what I suffer from. What about you? What do you feel like your problem is?"

"Killing."

Lashawn stopped dancing for a moment so she could look him over. "Are you serious?"

Macho nodded. "Yeah. Ever since I jumped off the porch, I've had this hatred and this pain inside me that I can't seem to conquer. My temper is horrible. I grew up watching my mom's get fucked over by man after man until finally she gave up on them altogether and started to date women. Most of the times I ran up on a nigga I imagined one of her boyfriends that used to beat on her and shit when I was too young to help her. So, yeah, my way of coping is killing and getting money. When you got money mafuckas love kissing your ass. That shit funny to me." He twirled her around and dipped her.

Lashawn came back up and wrapped her arm around his neck. "Macho, I can say that without a shadow of a doubt I love you with all my heart and soul. You have rescued me out of so many impossible situations that I know had you not, I woulda been dead already. With you, in my presence, I feel so much joy and determination. I am thankful for you, and I will love you until my last breath." She hugged him for a moment, took a deep breath, and slipped out of his arms with her back to him.

Macho watched her. "Baby, what's the matter?"

"Is there anything that you've wanted to tell me these last few months that you haven't been able to, huh?"

Macho felt sick on the stomach. "N'all, like what?"

"Are you absolutely sure? I mean, just wrack your brain for a minute, please, baby." Lashawn had her back turned to him with her shoulders slumped.

Macho stood stunned. "Yo', I would prefer for you to just holler at me. We are too old to be playing all that beat around the bush shit."

Lashawn turned back around with her eyes watery. She walked to the couch and grabbed her phone. She came back and handed it to him. "Watch this footage, Macho, and tell me what you think."

Macho grabbed her phone and started the video. It started gray and blurry at first. Then it got clear. It showed Pooh's G Wagon storming full speed into the dumpster at the Park View Apartment Complex it caught fire immediately. Seconds later

Macho pulled up and got out of his whip masked. He fired a series of shots bucking back to back. Then he jumped in his whip and headed out of the lot. He stopped, backed up, and went back to the scene and that's when Lashonda came out of the G Wagon on fire waving her little arms. She took five steps and fell lifeless to the ground. Macho stood over her in a panic. He looked both ways and took off running back into his whip where he fled the scene. The footage stopped. Macho was flabbergasted.

"I knew that if any nigga in the city was gon' get to Pooh and kill him that it was going to be you. I mean, after all, I truly believe that you love me. And when I told you that he raped me I saw the consequence of death for him in your eyes. Here's what I think. I think you found him, and you went to work on his ass as only you could. You didn't expect Lashonda to be in the Wagon with him. And when you found out that she was, you freaked. My only question to you is, when were you going to tell me about all this?"

Macho lowered his head. "Where did you get that footage?"

"It doesn't matter, Macho. What happened that night? Why did you do it?"

"What?" Macho eyed her closely. He took her blouse and ripped it down the middle looking for a wire. He saw none. He turned her around and forced her up against the wall, he searched her back and up and down her thighs. Then he grabbed her by the hair and pulled her into the bathroom where he turned on the sink water as high as he could. "Where did you get that footage Lashawn?"

"From the police nigga! Where the fuck else would I get it from. They said that this is the man that killed my daughter and my daughter's father. They told me to study it with everything that I had and when I was able to make out who he was to contact them."

"What is the detective's name?" He asked through clenched teeth, placing his forearm under her chin.

"Detective Wilson. His name is Wilson." She struggled to breathe.

"How much did you tell them? Huh, did you identify me?"

She shook her head. "N'all, I've been thinking about the pros and cons. Snitching on you can't bring my daughter back. Besides, I know you ain't do it on purpose. But why would you keep this away from me?"

Macho didn't trust her. He imagined going to prison for the rest of his life and he began to freak out. "Yo', that ain't me, Lashawn. I don't know who the fuck that was, but it wasn't me."

Lashawn mugged him. "You dirty son of a bitch! How dare you tell me a bald-faced lie. You don't think I know my man when I see him. That was you, and if you wanna play these games then maybe you ain't the man that I thought you were."

Macho's heart dropped. "Damn, Lashawn. Please don't make me do this."

"Get the fuck off me. I don't know who you are anymore. I don't trust you. George was right about you. He working with the police, too. Sho is, he already pointed you out and helped them track down this apartment camera footage. I guess he got caught stealing a car from that same parking lot a month ago and got flagged by the camera. He directed the police to it and well, here you are killing my baby. How dare you?"

"Damn, Lashawn." Macho lowered his head again. He grabbed her shirt in his hand and pulled his Glock-19 out.

Lashawn grew silent for a moment. "What are you doing, Macho?"

Macho began to cry. "I swear to God I love you, baby. I swear I feel like you are the only woman in this world for me. I woulda died for you, Lashawn."

Lashawn frowned and looked up at him. She held her head high. "So, now you gon' kill me like you did my daughter, huh? Well, go ahead, Macho. Send me with my baby so I can be with her again. Ain't much to this world no more no way. Stop saying that you love me. You took the only true love that I ever knew away from me. When I look at you all I see is hate. I'd be lying if I didn't admit that I wanna see you rot in hell. I can't love a man that I hate!" she screamed. "I lied to you anyway! Your brother gave me that shit!" She began to cry harder. "I'm dying anyway so kill me! Kill me you baby murder!"

Macho shook his head. He wiped away a tear, before flinging her into the bathtub. He pulled the shower curtain and fired all face shots, ten in a row. LaShawn's brains splattered all over the tiles and within the basin of the tub. As soon as he was done he kneeled on the side of the tub and dropped his gun crying his eyes out.

"Fuck! Dis was my bitch!" He lowered his head and cried into his hands for an hour.

Then he got up and chopped and burned her body. He spent the entire night cleaning up the crime scene before he burned the duplex to the ground starting with the bathroom.

***

Early the next morning, George woke up in his old run-down apartment and opened his eyes to find Macho standing over him with a black hoodie pulled over his head. He jumped and scurried back on the bed until his back was against the beat-up, old headboard. Roaches were crawling all over it. "M-M-Macho, what the fuck you doing in my house man?" George's eyes were bucked wide open.

Macho continued to stare at him. He took a deep breath and tried to keep his composure. "How long you been working wit' dem people snake ass nigga? And what all the fuck have you told them?"

"Dem people?" George laughed nervously. "What people are you talking about?" His heart began to pound in his chest. Sweat appeared on his brow suddenly.

Macho pulled his red rag up over his nose and came from behind his back with a hunting knife. The sharp ridges of the blade gleaned in the early sunlight that was coming from the window. "George, pussy ass nigga. I ain't got no time to be playin' wit' you. I need you to tell me everything you told the police." He lowered his head but kept his eyes on George the entire time.

George looked both ways for an exit. He thought about jumping out of the window, but he was on the fifth floor, there was a small chance that he would escape Macho and a larger chance that he would break his legs trying to do so. There had to be another way. He was starting to panic. "Look, man, they already knew about the Arab robbery. I just told them a little bit about that, but I kept yo' name out of it. I put it all on Preston, they don't even know that you were there," he lied, hating the police for not having picked up Macho and Preston already. *Didn't they know that every second that Macho and Preston walked the streets that I was in danger?* he thought. *Then again, this Baltimore and I'm black as oil, they probably didn't even care.*

"What about Pooh's shit? Why you tell them about all that bullshit? When you don't know anything. You sucka ass just ratting just to be ratting, huh?" Macho asked him this calmly, yet sinisterly.

"Fuck, aw man, that bitch Lashawn lying. I ain't told nobody you had nothing to do with Pooh's death. I told her that there was a camera in the parking lot cause that's how they caught me before when I stole a car from over that way. She said that she was going to talk to the manager to see if she could get the footage cause she felt like the police were taking too long to find out who killed Lashonda. Said cause she was a lil' black girl and Pooh was a known drug dealer that the police put them on the bottom of their list for justice.

"But first the lady didn't wanna help wit' the investigation, she said there was no footage until Lashawn gave her a thousand dollars. That's how Lashawn got the feed. Then Lashawn came and showed it to me, and asked me who it looked like, and I said you. I told *her* that, not no fuckin' police. She must've gone to them and I wouldn't put it past her either. You already know she probably jealous cause you fuck wit' so many hoez. Not to mention you were bogus for killing that girl and not telling her. Just my opinion, though."

Macho nodded. "Come here, nigga."

"Aw, why man?" He was terrified. He kept his eyes on the knife and he got up out of the bed real timid. He stepped in front of Macho but kept an arm's length distance. His body was bony with gray hair all over his chest. "I'd never wanna hurt you, Macho. Man, please believe me."

Macho reached and grabbed a hold of his shirt. He yanked him to him and leaned his face beside his ear. "My bitch say you gave her that pack you sick ass nigga. You passing that HIV bullshit around to our sistas? And cause of you and this rat shit I had to snuff my first love." George's eyes got big. Macho continued, "You ain't nothing but a bitch ass nigga. I hope you go straight to hell. All rats gotta die, George, even

146

Mickey Mouse." Macho took the blade and stabbed it into George's stomach as hard as he could then he pulled it upward giving him an autopsy style incision.

George gurgled on his own blood, screeched loudly, then fell backward with his intestines falling out of him. They dropped to the carpet like thick ropes of spaghetti. Blood bubbled out of his mouth. He tried to talk but failed.

Macho rushed him and slashed him across the face fifty times, spraying the walls. "You made me kill my bitch! You trying to set me up." He slashed him over and over. When George fell on his back, he straddled his chest and finished him off with a hundred grotesque stabs. Then he stood up and ordered his body snatchers to get rid of his body. Like LaShawn's place, he remained there for many hours cleaning the scene. His heart had never felt colder.

Ghost

Chapter 18

When Preston got back to Baltimore, he hit the ground running like never before. Phoenix sent him back home with fifty of his Duffel Bag Cartel savages, and though they were still technically under Phoenix. He gave them the order to fall under Preston and his subsection of the Cutthroat Mafia for one full year, or until further notice. They were tasked with security, hustling for Preston, and amongst other things to spy on the city of Baltimore and the Cutthroat Mafia. They were made to report back to Phoenix unbeknownst to Preston weekly with the latest developments.

Preston was oblivious to that fact. He set up shop in the Park View Apartments, and all up and down Colgate Avenue. He moved troops to West Baltimore, and all over Dundalk. Wherever Macho's portion of the Mafia was not he made sure that his was. He invaded project buildings and row houses, snatching up the youth there and employing them under his crew. He paid their parents rents, car notes, and put groceries in their homes for their cooperation and loyalty. Within three months, he had the city rocking and supplied them with the purest form of the Rebirth that was floating around the city like the Coronavirus.

Preston found himself so consumed with his hustling and the amount of money coming in that it took him nearly four months to take up the fact that he hadn't seen Lashawn or heard from her in that amount of time. When he'd hit up Macho, he was vague. He told him that Lashawn told him that she needed to go into a rehab where nobody had access to her because due to Lashonda's death and her house burning down, that she'd started to use a bunch of harmful drugs. Her house burning down was news to Preston. He wondered why she hadn't told him about it. She could have been seriously hurt.

He wondered if they were really that distant from each other. This hurt his heart.

Dope addicts throughout the city that were now copping the Rebirth exclusively from Preston's southern version of the Cutthroat Mafia confirmed that Lashawn had been using heroin like ninety going north. They also told him that she talked about going into rehab often. So, that checked out. When they told him that she'd been messing and sleeping around with George, Preston felt sick to his stomach. He took it upon himself to try and find George.

After two weeks of looking he could not. Once again, he looked to Macho for answers. Macho told him that he didn't fuck with George and that somebody told him that George had given some woman HIV and skipped town. He seemed disinterested in the topic of his brother, so Preston let it go. Two weeks after acquiring about George, a fisherman found George's head floating in the water around his boat while fishing on the creek.

When Preston told Macho about this all Macho said, *"Karma is a bitch."* Then asked him when they were going to touch base.

They set a date and time and Preston hung up the phone confused and worried for his sister. He'd not been able to locate the rehabilitation center that she'd been in and it scared him a bit. Macho wasn't much help. Something wasn't right and he needed to get to the bottom of it.

***

Three days later, Detective Wilson rolled up on Preston as he was coming out of Walmart one early Sunday morning. Because of the pandemic, Preston liked to get there early and shop along with the elderly. There was an older woman with-out any surviving family that stayed next door to his home in Dundalk by the name of Renee. He shopped for her every Sunday with her holding on to his right arm. While he used her as a beard to do his own shopping, he made it his business to take care of her as well. This day he'd just helped her get into the passenger's seat of his Bentley truck and closed the door when the Detective slid on him. Preston knew the man was with law enforcement right away because of the badge on his belt.

"Yo', I got two lawyers. Pick which one you wanna talk to, homeboy." Preston finished putting the bags in the truck, closed the back of it, and walked around to the driver's seat ready to close the door. When the Detective held it open. Preston mugged him. "Yo', I need to record this. You on some George Floyd shit? Breonna Taylor? What mafucka?"

"Calm down, Preston Miller. I ain't here to talk about the drug-dealing ring you're taking part in, or the kilos of dope we know is in your home, right now. Hell, I'm not even here to talk about that robbery you and Macho James did close to a year back. Nope, it's too cold out to talk about such things. And I definitely ain't trying to kill an unarmed person like yourself, right now. Even though I feel the world would be better off," he said this last part under his breath.

Preston's heart was beating fast. He continued to mug the officer. "Okay den, fuck is this a shakedown? How much you want, Swine?" He pulled out a twenty-thousand-dollar knot and thumbed through the bills. "What's your price?"

Detective Wilson laughed and turned his back to Preston. "When was the last time you saw fine ass, Lashawn? George even?"

Preston lowered the money. "You know where my sister is?"

Detective Wilson nodded. "Well, I might, and if you don't know then you are a damn fool. That's just what you are." Detective Wilson looked around the parking lot. "I think you need to come down to the station and talk to me one on one. Now I ain't looking to arrest you. I know you got a rap sheet long as Colgate Avenue and I ain't necessarily worried about it, right now. I'm more inclined to stop a tragic war that's coming to Baltimore if I don't intervene. With all this police defunding bull crap the mayor just doesn't know what's about to happen out here."

"Man, fuck that shit. What this have to do with my sister?" Preston snapped.

"Why don't you get your head out of your ass and come to see. Follow me." Detective Wilson began to walk toward his unmarked cruiser.

"N'all, I don't trust you bitchez. It's gon' take more than your pink ass to convince me to come to the sewers with you rats." He started the ignition of his Bentley ready to pull off.

Detective Wilson slammed his hand on the window seal. "What if I told you that your sister was dead and that we know who killed her?"

Preston's heart sank and he swallowed his spit. "*Dead!* Lashawn's dead. Yo', stop fuckin' wit' me. Where is my sister?" His eyes got watery.

"Follow me, I promise it'll be the best move you ever made." Detective Wilson walked away. "I'll get a car to take Renee home. Sides, you already used her this morning for *early bird* shopping." He looked back at Preston and shook his head.

"Fuck you, just hurry up. Yo', my sister bet not be dead." Imagining the possibility made him throw up in his mouth.

***

Macho was drunk, rolling off multiple pills and sitting at the bar of Dunbar's Tavern when he heard the door open, and heavy boots began to pile inside of the establishment. Macho took the shot of Grey Goose and downed it, tossing his head back, swallowing hard, slamming the glass on the counter. The liquor burned his throat. When he looked up to the bartender, he saw that the fat man's eyes were bucked wide open. Sweat appeared on the top of his bald head. He slowly backed away from the counter with his hands in the air. Macho's vision was slightly blurry, he was turnt up. He felt a heavy hand land on his shoulder, and then a shotgun entered into his right ear canal.

Kilroy leaned closer to him and put his lips right next to Macho's cheek. "I told you that I don't like to take no L's, didn't I, Macho?"

To Be Continued...
Cutthroat Mafia 3
Coming Soon

Submission Guideline

Submit the first three chapters of your completed manuscript to ldpsubmissions@gmail.com, subject line: Your book's title. The manuscript must be in a .doc file and sent as an attachment. Document should be in Times New Roman, double spaced and in size 12 font. Also, provide your synopsis and full contact information. If sending multiple submissions, they must each be in a separate email.

Have a story but no way to send it electronically? You can still submit to LDP/Ca$h Presents. Send in the first three chapters, written or typed, of your completed manuscript to:

**LDP: Submissions Dept
Po Box 944
Stockbridge, Ga 30281**

DO NOT send original manuscript. Must be a duplicate.

Provide your synopsis and a cover letter containing your full contact information.

Thanks for considering LDP and Ca$h Presents.

<u>Coming Soon from Lock Down Publications/Ca$h Presents</u>

BOW DOWN TO MY GANGSTA

By **Ca$h**

TORN BETWEEN TWO

By **Coffee**

THE STREETS STAINED MY SOUL **II**

By **Marcellus Allen**

BLOOD OF A BOSS **VI**

SHADOWS OF THE GAME II

By **Askari**

LOYAL TO THE GAME **IV**

By **T.J. & Jelissa**

A DOPEBOY'S PRAYER **II**

By **Eddie "Wolf" Lee**

IF LOVING YOU IS WRONG... **III**

By **Jelissa**

TRUE SAVAGE **VII**

MIDNIGHT CARTEL III

DOPE BOY MAGIC IV

CITY OF KINGZ II

By **Chris Green**

BLAST FOR ME **III**

A SAVAGE DOPEBOY III

CUTTHROAT MAFIA III

By **Ghost**

A HUSTLER'S DECEIT III

KILL ZONE **II**

BAE BELONGS TO ME III

A DOPE BOY'S QUEEN II

By **Aryanna**

COKE KINGS V

KING OF THE TRAP II

By **T.J. Edwards**

GORILLAZ IN THE BAY V

De'Kari

THE STREETS ARE CALLING II

Duquie Wilson

KINGPIN KILLAZ IV

STREET KINGS III

PAID IN BLOOD III

CARTEL KILLAZ IV

DOPE GODS III

Hood Rich

SINS OF A HUSTLA II

ASAD

KINGZ OF THE GAME V

Playa Ray

SLAUGHTER GANG IV

RUTHLESS HEART IV

By Willie Slaughter

THE HEART OF A SAVAGE III

By Jibril Williams

FUK SHYT II

By Blakk Diamond

FEAR MY GANGSTA 5

THE REALEST KILLAZ II

By Tranay Adams

TRAP GOD II

By Troublesome

YAYO IV

A SHOOTER'S AMBITION III

By S. Allen

GHOST MOB

Stilloan Robinson

KINGPIN DREAMS III

By Paper Boi Rari

CREAM

By Yolanda Moore

SON OF A DOPE FIEND III

By Renta

FOREVER GANGSTA II

GLOCKS ON SATIN SHEETS III

By Adrian Dulan

LOYALTY AIN'T PROMISED II

By Keith Williams

THE PRICE YOU PAY FOR LOVE II

DOPE GIRL MAGIC III

By Destiny Skai

CONFESSIONS OF A GANGSTA II

By Nicholas Lock

I'M NOTHING WITHOUT HIS LOVE II

By Monet Dragun

CAUGHT UP IN THE LIFE III

By Robert Baptiste

LIFE OF A SAVAGE IV

A GANGSTA'S QUR'AN II

MURDA SEASON II

By **Romell Tukes**

QUIET MONEY III

THUG LIFE II

By **Trai'Quan**

THE STREETS MADE ME III

By **Larry D. Wright**

THE ULTIMATE SACRIFICE VI

IF YOU CROSS ME ONCE II

ANGEL III

By **Anthony Fields**

THE LIFE OF A HOOD STAR

By Ca$h & Rashia Wilson

FRIEND OR FOE II

By **Mimi**

SAVAGE STORMS II

By **Meesha**

BLOOD ON THE MONEY II

By J-Blunt

Available Now

RESTRAINING ORDER **I & II**

By **CA$H & Coffee**

LOVE KNOWS NO BOUNDARIES **I II & III**

By **Coffee**

RAISED AS A GOON I, II, III & IV

BRED BY THE SLUMS I, II, III

BLAST FOR ME I & II

ROTTEN TO THE CORE I II III

A BRONX TALE I, II, III

DUFFEL BAG CARTEL I II III IV

HEARTLESS GOON I II III IV

A SAVAGE DOPEBOY I II

HEARTLESS GOON I II III

DRUG LORDS I II III

CUTTHROAT MAFIA I II

By **Ghost**

LAY IT DOWN **I & II**

LAST OF A DYING BREED

BLOOD STAINS OF A SHOTTA I & II III

By **Jamaica**

LOYAL TO THE GAME I II III

LIFE OF SIN I, II III

Ghost

PUSH IT TO THE LIMIT

By **Bre' Hayes**

BLOOD OF A BOSS **I, II, III, IV, V**

SHADOWS OF THE GAME

By **Askari**

THE STREETS BLEED MURDER **I, II & III**

THE HEART OF A GANGSTA I II& III

By **Jerry Jackson**

CUM FOR ME I II III IV V

An **LDP Erotica Collaboration**

BRIDE OF A HUSTLA **I II & II**

THE FETTI GIRLS **I, II& III**

CORRUPTED BY A GANGSTA I, II III, IV

BLINDED BY HIS LOVE

THE PRICE YOU PAY FOR LOVE

DOPE GIRL MAGIC I II

By **Destiny Skai**

WHEN A GOOD GIRL GOES BAD

By **Adrienne**

THE COST OF LOYALTY I II III

By Kweli

A GANGSTER'S REVENGE **I II III & IV**

THE BOSS MAN'S DAUGHTERS I II III IV V

A SAVAGE LOVE **I & II**

BAE BELONGS TO ME I II

A HUSTLER'S DECEIT I, II, III

WHAT BAD BITCHES DO I, II, III

SOUL OF A MONSTER I II III
KILL ZONE
A DOPE BOY'S QUEEN
By **Aryanna**
A KINGPIN'S AMBITON
A KINGPIN'S AMBITION **II**
I MURDER FOR THE DOUGH
By **Ambitious**
TRUE SAVAGE I II III IV V VI
DOPE BOY MAGIC I, II, III
MIDNIGHT CARTEL I II
CITY OF KINGZ
By **Chris Green**
A DOPEBOY'S PRAYER
By **Eddie "Wolf" Lee**
THE KING CARTEL **I, II & III**
By **Frank Gresham**
THESE NIGGAS AIN'T LOYAL **I, II & III**
By **Nikki Tee**
GANGSTA SHYT **I II &III**
By **CATO**
THE ULTIMATE BETRAYAL
By **Phoenix**
BOSS'N UP **I , II & III**
By **Royal Nicole**
I LOVE YOU TO DEATH
By **Destiny J**

I RIDE FOR MY HITTA

I STILL RIDE FOR MY HITTA

By **Misty Holt**

LOVE & CHASIN' PAPER

By **Qay Crockett**

TO DIE IN VAIN

SINS OF A HUSTLA

By **ASAD**

BROOKLYN HUSTLAZ

By **Boogsy Morina**

BROOKLYN ON LOCK I & II

By **Sonovia**

GANGSTA CITY

By **Teddy Duke**

A DRUG KING AND HIS DIAMOND I & II III

A DOPEMAN'S RICHES

HER MAN, MINE'S TOO I, II

CASH MONEY HO'S

By Nicole Goosby

TRAPHOUSE KING **I II & III**

KINGPIN KILLAZ I II III

STREET KINGS I II

PAID IN BLOOD **I II**

CARTEL KILLAZ I II III

DOPE GODS I II

By **Hood Rich**

LIPSTICK KILLAH **I, II, III**

CRIME OF PASSION I II & III

FRIEND OR FOE

By **Mimi**

STEADY MOBBN' **I, II, III**

THE STREETS STAINED MY SOUL

By **Marcellus Allen**

WHO SHOT YA **I, II, III**

SON OF A DOPE FIEND I II

Renta

GORILLAZ IN THE BAY **I II III IV**

TEARS OF A GANGSTA I II

DE'KARI

TRIGGADALE I II III

Elijah R. Freeman

GOD BLESS THE TRAPPERS I, II, III

THESE SCANDALOUS STREETS I, II, III

FEAR MY GANGSTA I, II, III IV

THESE STREETS DON'T LOVE NOBODY I, II

BURY ME A G I, II, III, IV, V

A GANGSTA'S EMPIRE I, II, III, IV

THE DOPEMAN'S BODYGAURD I II

THE REALEST KILLAZ

Tranay Adams

THE STREETS ARE CALLING

Duquie Wilson

MARRIED TO A BOSS... I II III

By Destiny Skai & Chris Green

KINGZ OF THE GAME I II III IV

Playa Ray

SLAUGHTER GANG I II III

RUTHLESS HEART I II III

By Willie Slaughter

FUK SHYT

By Blakk Diamond

DON'T F#CK WITH MY HEART I II

By Linnea

ADDICTED TO THE DRAMA I II III

By Jamila

YAYO I II III

A SHOOTER'S AMBITION I II

By S. Allen

TRAP GOD

By Troublesome

FOREVER GANGSTA

GLOCKS ON SATIN SHEETS I II

By Adrian Dulan

TOE TAGZ I II III

By Ah'Million

KINGPIN DREAMS I II

By Paper Boi Rari

CONFESSIONS OF A GANGSTA

By Nicholas Lock

I'M NOTHING WITHOUT HIS LOVE

By Monet Dragun

Ghost

CAUGHT UP IN THE LIFE I II

By Robert Baptiste

NEW TO THE GAME I II III

By **Malik D. Rice**

LIFE OF A SAVAGE I II III

A GANGSTA'S QUR'AN

MURDA SEASON

By **Romell Tukes**

LOYALTY AIN'T PROMISED

By Keith Williams

QUIET MONEY I II

THUG LIFE

By **Trai'Quan**

THE STREETS MADE ME I II

By **Larry D. Wright**

THE ULTIMATE SACRIFICE I, II, III, IV, V

KHADIFI

IF YOU CROSS ME ONCE

ANGEL I II

By **Anthony Fields**

THE LIFE OF A HOOD STAR

By Ca$h & Rashia Wilson

BOOKS BY LDP'S CEO, CA$H

TRUST IN NO MAN

TRUST IN NO MAN 2

TRUST IN NO MAN 3

BONDED BY BLOOD

SHORTY GOT A THUG

THUGS CRY

THUGS CRY 2

THUGS CRY 3

TRUST NO BITCH

TRUST NO BITCH 2

TRUST NO BITCH 3

TIL MY CASKET DROPS

RESTRAINING ORDER

RESTRAINING ORDER 2

IN LOVE WITH A CONVICT

LIFE OF A HOOD STAR

Coming Soon

BONDED BY BLOOD 2

BOW DOWN TO MY GANGSTA

Ghost